Even in human form, Rafe terrified me with all the unleashed power I felt emanating from him. I didn't know why he'd only recently started drawing my attention—although *draw* was too tame a word. I couldn't go five seconds without thinking about him, without looking around to see where he was. I was curious about him in ways I'd never been about any other guy, not even Connor—Connor, who had been chosen as my mate.

I wanted to know the kinds of movies Rafe enjoyed and what books he read. But most of all I wanted to know what it felt like to have him wrap his arms around me the way he had in the dream.

"Only about two more weeks and we get to play with the big boys," Brittany whispered, breaking the spell Rafe held over me and igniting a spark of guilt within.

RACHEL HAWTHORNE

FULL MOON

A DARK GUARDIAN NOVEL

HARPER TEEN

An imprint of HarperCollins*Publishers*

HarperTeen is an imprint of HarperCollins Publishers.

Dark Guardian: Full Moon
Copyright © 2009 by Jan L. Nowasky
www.harperteen.com

Library of Congress Cataloging-in-Publication Data
Hawthorne, Rachel.
    Full moon / Rachel Hawthorne. — 1st ed.
        p.   cm. — (Dark Guardian ; #2)
    "A Dark Guardian novel."
    Summary: As the time for her transformation draws near and a
deadly threat to the Dark Guardians escalates, Lindsey finds herself
increasingly captivated by Rafe despite her long-standing commitment to Connor.
    ISBN 978-0-06-170956-2 (pbk. bdg.)
    [1. Supernatural—Fiction.   2. Werewolves—Fiction.   3. For-
ests and forestry—Fiction.]   I. Title.
PZ7.H31374Ful 2009   2009005243
[Fic]—dc22   CIP
                                                        AC

Typography by Andrea Vandergrift
09   10   11   12   13   LP/RRDH   10 9 8 7 6 5 4 3 2 1

❖
First Edition

For Brandon,
paranormal advisor extraordinaire.
Thanks for all the breakfast brainstorming sessions
and letting me bounce various scenarios off you.
You're terrific! Love, Mom

PROLOGUE

The full moon has become my enemy.

I'm in a cavern, preparing myself for the most important night of my life. A few days earlier I had turned seventeen. Tonight a full moon will grace the sky. As I stand beneath it, the moonlight will wash over me and I—Lindsey Lancaster—will transform. . . .

Into a wolf.

I'm a Shifter, a species of beings who for thousands of years have possessed the ability to shift from human to animal form. My clan's destined animal is the wolf.

For as long as I can remember I've been anxiously awaiting this night, but for the past few weeks I've been dreading its arrival, because things suddenly became very confusing and complicated. My feelings, my emotions—they were all over the place. My heart was telling me one thing, my head another.

Connor and I have been best friends forever. Our families always hang out together in the outside world, where we all pretend that we don't have this amazing ability, where we pretend we're like the Statics, those who can't morph into another shape. Our parents are convinced that Connor and I are destined for each other.

Sometimes I fear that Connor and I got caught up in *their* dreams for us and decided those dreams were ours, too. One night, in front of everyone, Connor declared me his mate. I was thrilled that he held such intense feelings for me, because I thought I felt the same for him. Our families celebrated. In the tradition of our kind, he had my name tattooed in a Celtic symbol on his left shoulder—our equivalent of getting engaged. Our fate was sealed.

But then Rafe returned home this summer after a year away at college, and I began to notice him in ways I never had before. When he speaks, his deep voice is laced with a little bit of a rasp—so sexy. He doesn't talk often, except when he has something important to say, and when he does, my toes tingle. His dark eyes have the ability to hold me captive, to make my heart beat like thunder. And when he drops that dangerous gaze to my lips, I want to melt into his arms and pull his mouth down to mine for a taste of the forbidden.

He possesses a wild streak, prefers to live life on the edge. He's the big, bad wolf—pardon the pun. And something in him calls to the wildness in me . . . but it's a call I can't answer.

Connor is my destiny.

Two years older than I am, he's already gone through his transformation. Tonight he'll lead me through mine. I force myself to concentrate on Connor: his blond hair, his blue eyes, his crooked grin that always makes me smile. He's waiting for me now, waiting to share the most important night of my life. He'll hold me, guide me through the transition, and ensure that I survive. We'll bond deeply and forever as we go through this experience together. That's what is supposed to happen, anyway.

I study my reflection in the mirror. My eyes are hazel, although the color tends to shift with my mood. Tonight they look somehow more blue than green or brown. They're sad when they should be filled with excitement at this moment, the kind of anticipation a girl feels right before the prom.

My white-blond hair hangs loosely around my shoulders. The white velvet robe I'm wearing caresses my bare skin, and nervousness descends as I realize that soon it will be the moonlight touching me—the moonlight and Connor.

I turn from the mirror and walk to the entrance of the cavern, where a cascading waterfall hides our lair from those who don't know of its—of *our*—existence. I slip out from behind the curtain of water and circle the still pool that will soon reflect the rising moon.

I spy Connor waiting patiently for my arrival. Wearing a black robe, he holds out his hand, and I place my palm against his. His fingers—so long, so sure, so steady— close around mine, which suddenly seem too delicate and fragile for what is about to happen. As though sensing my apprehension, he draws me near. The familiarity of him gives me solace. He's *the one*. He's always been the one.

Leaning in, he brushes his lips over mine. My heart stutters with the enormity of what we're about to do.

Holding my hand, he leads me toward the clearing, toward the waiting moon, toward forever as his mate.

And I just hope that I haven't made the wrong choice. Otherwise, I'm walking straight into the single biggest mistake of my life.

ONE

Supposedly, dreams reflect our hidden fears and secret desires, all clamoring for attention. The one I'd had last night had been so vivid that even now, as evening drew near, it still made me squirm in my chair. I sat against a wall in the counsel room where the elders and the Dark Guardians—protectors of our society—were discussing how best to ensure our survival. Because I hadn't yet experienced my first transformation, I was considered a novice and was not allowed to sit at the large, round table with the others. This was okay by me, because it gave me the freedom to let my mind wander—without anyone noticing that I wasn't paying attention.

In my dream, I'd been standing in a clearing with my declared mate, Connor, our arms wrapped around each other so tightly that we could barely breathe. The full moon served as a spotlight.

Then dark clouds drifted over the moon, and everything went black. Still holding him near, I was acutely aware of the muscles and bones in his body undulating against me. He grew taller and broader. My fingers were in his hair, and I felt the strands thicken and lengthen. His mouth covered mine, but his lips were fuller than before. The kiss was hungrier than any he'd ever given me. It heated me from head to toe, and I thought I knew what it was to be a candle, melting from the scorching flame. I knew I should move away, but I clung to him as though I'd drown in a sea of doubts if I let go.

The hovering clouds floated away, and the moonlight illuminated us once again—only I was no longer in Connor's arms. Instead I was pressing my body against Rafe's, kissing him, yearning for his touch. . . .

I shifted uncomfortably in my chair with the memory of how desperately I'd wanted Rafe. It was Connor I was supposed to long for. But I'd woken up in a tangle of sheets, clamoring for another of Rafe's touches—even if it were only in a dream.

Squirming again, I felt a sharp elbow in my ribs.

"Be still, will you?" Brittany Reed whispered harshly

beside me. Like me, she would soon be turning seventeen and would experience her first transformation with the next full moon.

I'd known Brittany since kindergarten. We were friends, but I'd never felt as close to her as I did to Kayla—whom I'd met only last summer, when her adoptive parents had brought her to the park to face her past. We'd connected on a deep level almost as soon as we met. We'd spent the past year sharing our lives through emails, text messages, and phone calls.

During the last full moon she'd discovered that she was one of us and that Lucas Wilde was her destined mate. I can't imagine how frightening it would be to have so little time to prepare. We Shifters can't control the first transformation. When the full moon rises, our bodies react to its call. But now Kayla sat at the table with the others.

The summer solstice, the longest day of the year, is usually a time when as many of our kind as possible come together to celebrate our existence. But this year a pall hung over us as we gathered at Wolford, a village hidden deep within a huge national forest near the Canadian border. All that remained there of what had once been a vibrant community were a few small buildings and the massive, mansionlike structure that serves as the home of the elders who rule over us. The residence also houses most of us when we're here for the solstice celebration.

We've always been a secret society. Even though we have lived among the rest of the world, we show our true selves only to each other. But recently, we discovered that Lucas's older brother had betrayed us by telling someone in the outside world about our existence. Now some scientists who work for a medical research company called Bio-Chrome were determined to capture us and discover what makes us tick—or more important, what makes us transform. They wanted to patent this ability, develop it, and use it for their own financial gain. But being dissected and studied wasn't how any of us wanted to spend our summer vacation.

Although we hadn't seen any signs of Bio-Chrome scientists since Lucas and Kayla had escaped from their clutches, none of us believed they'd given up their quest so easily. We were all on edge because we could sense an impending confrontation—the way animals sense a coming storm. Nature had made us attuned to danger. It was the reason we hadn't gone the way of the dinosaur.

Brittany was right. I needed to keep calm. I had to stop thinking about that crazy dream and pay more attention to the discussion at the table. Unfortunately as my gaze wandered around the group, it slammed into Rafe's. He was watching me with an intensity that made me think he knew about my unsettling dream. His dark eyes held a challenge, dared me not to look away, tempted me to risk getting caught staring at him instead of concentrating on protecting us from Bio-Chrome. At that particular moment, though, I didn't believe any scientist was more dangerous to me than Rafe.

He studied me with single-minded purpose. I could almost feel the touch of his gaze on my skin. I knew I should look away, but I didn't want to lose this powerful connection. I'd never felt anything quite this intense before. The edges of my vision blurred; the words being spoken came to me distorted, as though I were underwater. My heart was speeding up one second, slowing down the next—it was as confused as I was. I wanted to stand up and walk over to him. I wanted to run from the room.

Rafe never talked much during these sessions—but then, he never spoke much at all. He was Lucas's second in command, more about actions than words. He always looked as though he'd forgotten to shave that morning, with just the barest hint of sexy stubble on his chin. His thick, straight hair brushed along his shoulders and was the black of a moonless night, nearly matching eyes the shade of hot fudge. When he transformed, he was gorgeous . . . and lethal.

Last summer I'd seen him take out a cougar when we'd been scouting an area before taking some campers there. The cougar had attacked, Rafe had shifted, and I'd seen firsthand what our kind is capable of when threatened. We are aggressive and deadly.

Even in human form, Rafe terrified me with all the unleashed power I felt emanating from him. I didn't know why he'd only recently started drawing my attention—although *draw* was too tame a word. I couldn't go five seconds without thinking about him, without looking around to see where he was. I was curious about him in ways I'd never been about any other guy, not even Connor. I wanted to know the kinds of movies he enjoyed and what books he read. I wanted to listen to his iPod playlist and discover his favorite music. But most of all I wanted to know what it felt like to have him wrap his arms around me the way he had in the dream. I wanted to experience the heat of his kiss.

"Only about two more weeks and we get to play with the big boys," Brittany whispered, breaking the spell Rafe held over me and igniting a spark of guilt within. Had she noticed where my attention had been drawn, which "big boy" held me enthralled? Or had she been searching the table, too, hoping to catch someone's attention? Legend had it that a girl couldn't survive the first transformation if she went through it alone.

"Aren't you scared?" I asked. "I mean, since no one has declared you yet." As soon as I said it, I was shocked at myself. Brittany was probably worrying plenty about it without a harsh reminder from me.

But she just rolled her deep blue eyes and tossed her head, flicking the thick braid of coal-black hair over her shoulder. "That is so medieval. I shouldn't have to wait for a guy to get off his butt and approach me. If he's the one I want, I should be able to *ask him*. Nothing wrong with being a little alpha-female. This is the twenty-first century, after all."

"So who would you ask—if it were allowed?"

She hesitated, and for a brief second I thought she was going to give me a name, but then she just shrugged as though she hadn't made up her mind. "Someone my parents didn't shove down my throat."

Ouch! I knew she was referring to how my parents and Connor's had sort of pushed us together. "My parents didn't choose Connor."

"Get real. Family vacations, gymnastics, birthday parties—your family had you doing everything together from the time you were born."

I couldn't argue with the truth. Connor had always been there for all the big moments of my life. I had photographs of Connor and me dropping through the Tower of Terror at Disney World, boogie boarding in the Hawaii surf, skiing the backwoods in Aspen. . . . The list went on. We'd spent many a summer screaming and laughing as we rode the daredevil rides and enjoyed the local attractions wherever our parents took us for vacation. I remembered how lonely I'd been on vacation when I was fifteen and he'd spent his first summer and winter break working in the national forest as a sherpa—our name for those who guide campers into the heart of the wilderness and ensure they come nowhere near our hidden sites. The next summer I'd applied for the sherpa program.

"We always had fun together," I told Brittany now. "We're compatible."

"Compatible? Makes it sound like you're picking out shoes to wear with a new skirt. Accepting your mate is probably the single most important decision you'll ever make in your life."

"Why are you questioning my choice?" *And making me question my choice in the process,* I thought. Or was it the dream creating these stupid doubts?

"Because it's not fair to Connor if you don't truly love him."

"And how is any of this your business?" I retorted. Her mouth straightened into a flat line. She'd been hassling me about my relationship with Connor since summer began, insinuating that I wasn't a good girlfriend. "Oh my God. Are *you* in love with him?"

Before she could answer—assuming she would have done so—Lucas Wilde, our pack leader, twisted around from his place at the table and glared at us. Silently chastised, I pressed my lips together, gave him a nod, and finally concentrated on what was being discussed at the table. After our transformations, Brittany and I would bring the number of Dark Guardians to twelve. But Kayla, Lucas, Connor, Rafe, Brittany, and I were a sherpa team. We worked together to take campers into the wilderness. Serving as guides was how we'd met the Bio-Chrome group and become aware of its true purpose.

"I don't see that there's much we can do at this point," Connor was saying, and I experienced a prickle of pride that he wasn't afraid to speak up to the three elders who sat together, forming a chain of wisdom and history. "Dr. Keane and his team left the forest two weeks ago. Maybe they've given up their search for us by now."

Dr. Keane was the lead scientist at Bio-Chrome and one of the masterminds behind the plan to study us. The other was his son, Mason.

"But they're probably just regrouping. I wouldn't be surprised if they show up again any day now," Lucas said.

"I agree," Kayla said.

Lucas gave her a warm smile and, out of sight of the elders, took her hand beneath the table. With her red hair flowing around her shoulders, she would have stood out anyway, but the way she glowed with Lucas's attention made her stunning.

"Believe me, Mason is obsessed with capturing one

of us and discovering the key to our ability to transform. They're going to come back, so we need to be ready," she continued. "He's not going to give up."

For a while, at the beginning of the summer, Kayla had been interested in Mason—maybe as a potential boyfriend. Needless to say, her interest had come to a screeching halt when she discovered that in Mason's eyes, she was the bait to trap Lucas. It was impossible to envision her with anyone other than Lucas now.

Elder Wilde, Lucas's grandfather, stood. "We will remain alert. Our lives are dependent upon the skills and cunning of our Dark Guardians. I have complete faith in your abilities to protect us. Now it is time to celebrate the summer solstice, as many of our kind have come here for that purpose." He spread his arms as though he'd embrace us all. "Forget our troubles. Enjoy the night."

"He's kidding, right?" Brittany asked beneath her breath.

"Elder Wilde hasn't met Mason and his dad. He doesn't understand how truly dangerous or obsessed they are," I responded.

"Do you really think it can be done? The creation of a serum that will cause lycanthropy?"

"I don't know. But it's not like there's a virus running through our blood. It's genetic. You either have the gene or you don't."

"Yeah," Brittany mumbled. "Tough on those who don't."

"At least we don't have to worry about that. Soon we'll be shifting along with the best of them." I stood up and stepped away from her as Kayla approached, smiling brightly, her pale blue eyes radiating excitement.

"So what were you two gossiping about over here? I was feeling totally left out."

"Nothing important," I told her.

"See, that just proves my point," Brittany said.

Her point being that I hadn't given enough thought to selecting my mate. I was starting to get annoyed with this line of thought. She really needed to change her tune. Maybe if she wasn't so obsessed with my choice, she'd find a guy of her own.

"What point?" Connor asked as he came to stand beside me. I stiffened, wondering how he'd react to Brittany's accusations that we were forced together by our parents.

But she just said, "It's nothing."

I relaxed. She wasn't going to reveal her opinion that my feelings toward Connor weren't sincere. I didn't want him to doubt my affections, because I did care about him—no matter what Brittany thought. Connor and I had always known we belonged together.

Lucas came up behind Kayla, put his arm around her,

and drew her up against his side as though he couldn't stand not touching her. Why didn't Connor and I possess this crazy urge to snuggle all the time?

Self-consciously, I did a quick search around the room and discovered that Rafe had already left. I wasn't surprised. Unless we were all working, partying, or protecting the pack together, he was a loner.

"So are we ready to hit the party?" Lucas asked.

"Are you kidding? This is my first summer solstice celebration. I want to dress up a little," Kayla said.

His gaze swept over her. "I think you look good now."

"Has he ever got the boyfriend moves down," Brittany said, with teasing in her voice.

I turned my attention to Connor. "I'm going to change clothes, too."

"Okay. I'll find you."

How different his tone was from Lucas's! I told myself it was because Lucas and Kayla had only just discovered each other, while Connor and I had been together forever. Even so, I couldn't help but believe we should still feel that spark of excitement when we were near each other.

"I can't get over how immense this place is," Kayla said as we walked down the hallway toward the foyer, having left the guys in the counsel room. Everything I took for granted was new to her. It made me view things through fresh eyes.

All the walls were paneled in dark wood. The stone floor was worn and scratched in places where claws had traveled over it. Portraits of our ancestors, in both human and wolf forms, lined the walls.

"The whole clan used to live here," Brittany said. She enjoyed our history, while usually I could take it or leave it. "We were self-sufficient. Then industrialization began to take hold, and we realized how much we'd miss out on if we continued to isolate ourselves."

"So out into the big, bad world we went," I interjected.

"It's not that bad," Brittany said.

"Then why do we have to keep our existence a secret?" I asked.

"Because when we tried to reveal ourselves, we were tortured and burned as witches or demons," Brittany answered.

"I know that happened a long time ago," Kayla said. "But don't you think people are more enlightened these days?"

"What was your gut reaction when you learned that we existed?" I asked.

She blushed so deeply that the light smattering of freckles across her cheeks disappeared. "Astounded. And

I hate to admit it, but I was horrified when I discovered I was one of you. But now that I understand we're not rabid werewolves with evil intentions, I think it's pretty cool. That's all I'm saying. If people were given a chance to understand what we truly are, they might accept us."

"Or they might want to capture and study us. Like Bio-Chrome."

"But if people knew about us, the government would protect us."

"We protect ourselves," Brittany said vehemently. "We always have. We always will."

"I just think that having some help isn't such a bad idea."

"It's not our decision to make," I said as we neared the grand, sweeping staircase that would take us up to the room we were sharing. "Besides, we have way more important decisions to face—like what we're going to wear tonight."

TWO

Unlike Kayla, I had attended many summer solstice celebrations. They were characterized by an abundance of food and out-of-date music that our parents would dance to—and that we wouldn't be caught dead even listening to. Those around my age would gather mostly in small groups to talk, while avoiding the older members who were prone to pinching our cheeks and reminding us how cute we used to be.

"So how do I dress for this thing?" Kayla asked as she scrounged through her small duffle bag.

"Sexy," I said as I pulled a red spaghetti-strap tank out of my bag. The nights grow cool this far north, so I planned to wear a white denim jacket over it.

I walked into the bathroom where, at the long counter, Brittany was already straightening her black hair with a flat iron. When we were hiking through the woods, we usually wore our hair pulled back or braided—anything to minimize tangles. Tonight, though, I was going to leave my white-blond hair flowing around my shoulders.

I leaned toward the mirror and applied mascara. My skin had a healthy glow from all the time I spent outdoors. Anticipation of the evening had turned my hazel eyes a little greener.

"Do weird activities go on during this summer solstice thing? Do I need to be prepared for anything? I mean, the guys don't all strip down and transform do they?" Kayla asked as she came into the bathroom wearing a denim skirt and a cute, lacy pink top.

"I wish," Brittany mumbled. "I think they look best when they're in wolf form."

"Really?" I asked.

"Yeah, don't you?"

I thought about it for a moment. What she'd said seemed momentous somehow, but I couldn't figure out why. It was as though she viewed us somehow differently than most Shifters viewed ourselves. "No, they look the same to me, in whichever form they're in. What do you think, Kayla?"

"I don't really prefer one over the other, I guess. Lucas is Lucas, no matter what. It's just a shape."

"Exactly," I said.

"Maybe you two just don't appreciate the wolf as much as you should," Brittany said with a hint of tartness in her voice. "I'm outta here."

She strode out of the room. Kayla raised an eyebrow at me. I shrugged. "She's in a strange mood."

Kayla wrinkled her brow. "Do you ever get the sense that she's . . ." Her voice trailed off.

"That's she's what?"

"I don't know. Different. I feel connected to you, like there's a natural bond between us, but I don't feel that way with Brittany."

It made me feel disloyal to Brittany to admit that sometimes I did get strange vibes from her. "You just haven't known her long enough."

"I guess so."

When Kayla was ready, we went outside to where the festivities would take place. Beef was being cooked slowly over a large pit. Assorted vegetables and desserts were spread out on several tables. People walked around, eating and talking.

"It's kinda like a big company picnic or something," Kayla said.

"Family reunion, in a way, I guess. We might not be

directly related through blood, but we're related through an ancient curse."

"You really think the first wolf was the result of a curse?"

"Maybe."

"Lucas thinks we've been around since the dawn of time."

"That's a possibility, too, I guess. Brittany would probably know. She studies all that history stuff."

"What stuff?" Connor asked as he and Lucas joined us. Connor closed his hand around mine. It had been forever since we'd held hands. I wondered if he'd noticed the closeness between Kayla and Lucas, too. A soft, hunter green shirt was tucked into his dark jeans. He looked great.

"Where we came from," I said.

"The ancient text says we've always existed," Lucas said as he slipped his arm around Kayla's waist and drew her against his side.

"An ancient text that's for our eyes only?" Kayla asked, gazing up at him with an expression of adoration. It was so obvious that they were right for each other.

"For the elders. It's kept in a special room." Lucas tilted his head to the side. "Come on, let's go to the party."

I started to follow, but Connor held me back with a slight tug on my hand.

"Think he wants to show her around," he said. "Privately." His tone was suggestive.

"Oh. Right." I couldn't help but feel a pang of jealousy. Kayla and Lucas could barely keep their hands off each other, while Connor and I just acted like old buddies.

He gave me a warm smile of approval. "You look nice."

"Are you saying I don't usually?" I teased.

"You always look great. You know that. It's one of the reasons Rafe can't keep his eyes off you."

I felt my stomach knot and wondered if he'd noticed that lately I was having a difficult time keeping my eyes off Rafe. "I hadn't noticed," I lied.

"Good thing I know you're mine or I might get jealous," he said.

Secretly I wondered if a little jealousy would be a good thing. I wanted to feel that spark between us that was so obvious between Kayla and Lucas.

"Come on. Let's grab something to eat," Connor said, still holding my hand and pulling me along as he raced toward the grill. I couldn't help but giggle at his enthusiasm. How many times over the years had we hurried someplace because he was hungry?

After piling our plates with meat that had been cooked just enough that the blood running off it was warm,

Connor and I settled on the ground beneath a tree, eating in companionable silence.

"Is it just me or does something seem to be missing this year?" I asked after a while.

"Yeah, something is definitely missing. It's called laughter."

Once he said it, I knew he was right. "So do you think this Bio-Chrome thing is really a problem?" I asked, hoping he would say *no*.

"I'm afraid so. I don't think they're going to give up." He paused. "But we have to go back to business as usual, bringing campers into the forest. We just have to be aware that some campers might be their spies."

I thought about this for a moment. "Do you think they suspect that anyone in our group other than Lucas is a Shifter?"

"Hard to say."

"I really think Mason may have grown up reading too many comic books. He probably believes being bitten by a radioactive spider will turn him into Spider-Man."

Connor grinned. "It won't?"

Playfully, I slapped his arm. He's big into superheroes. Iron Man is his favorite, because he doesn't actually possess superpowers. All of a sudden it seemed strange to me that Connor would prefer the guy who, without his metal suit, was as "normal" as the majority of the world.

"Are you comfortable being a Shifter?" I blurted out.

"Never really thought about it. Why?"

"Just thinking about how you admire Iron Man. I should probably leave the psychoanalysis to the pros."

"Definitely."

My thoughts shifted back to Bio-Chrome. "Maybe *we* should put a spy in *their* camp."

Connor stared at me.

"What?" I asked, uncomfortable with his intensity.

"That's not a bad idea."

"I was kidding. Besides, who'd be crazy enough to volunteer?"

"Someone who thought they had nothing to lose."

"Brittany, maybe," I said quietly. I touched his knee. "Connor, you pal around with the guys. Why doesn't anyone show an interest in her?"

He slowly shook his head. "Who the hell knows? There's just something about her."

I furrowed my brow. "What do you mean?"

Sighing, he took a bite of meat and chewed for a while, as though he had to digest his thoughts. "It's hard to explain. She's hot—and in shape. I mean, man, she runs a couple of miles before dawn each morning, plus she does all those push-ups and sit-ups and even some weight training—which I've always thought is kind of weird for a girl because we're genetically prone to be in amazing shape. So why the workouts?"

"You work out," I reminded him.

"Yeah, but it's different for guys. It's because we're guys."

"Girls work out, too."

"But not with the intensity that Brittany does."

He stopped for a moment, grasping for words. "But it's more than that with her. I look at you and I feel a soul-deep connection. Wolf to wolf. Even when I met Kayla, I felt that *zing* that meant she's one of us. But with Brittany, there's nothing. It's like seeing some of the Static girls on campus and just knowing they're outsiders."

"But Brittany *is* one of us," I insisted.

"I know. It makes no sense, but I'm not the only guy who feels Static vibes coming off her."

"But she can't be a Static. Her parents are Shifters." They had to be. I knew her mother. As for her dad, I'd never met him. No one had as far as I knew. He lived in Europe, part of another clan. It had always been just Brittany and her mom. But still, I couldn't imagine that her mom would hook up with a non-Shifter. I wasn't even sure that was possible. "She'd have to be some kind of mutation or something." I shook my head, totally blown away by the concept, and repeated, "She's one of us."

"Hey, Connor!" one of the guys called out, interrupting our discussion about Brittany. Not that I thought we had much more to say on the subject. The very idea of her not being a Shifter was too weird even to contemplate. As far as I knew, nothing like that had ever happened. "The old men are challenging us to a game of tag football. Fathers against sons. You in?"

"You bet."

"Meet us in five. In the clearing." He raced off.

"You gonna watch us play?" Connor asked.

"Sure."

"Give me a kiss for good luck?"

I gave him what I hoped was a sexy grin. "Like you have to ask."

He leaned in and kissed me. I'm always amazed by how warm his mouth is, by how nice it feels to be kissed by Connor. Not that I had any other experience to compare it to—he'd always been my one and only.

Drawing back, he smiled broadly. "I want more of that after I whip my dad's butt."

I laughed as he pulled me to my feet. We dropped our plates off and headed over to the clearing. He gave me another quick kiss before loping into the area where Lucas and several other Dark Guardians were waiting for him. Connor was incredibly swift and graceful. I loved watching the way he moved. He was amazingly perfect.

I thought about looking for Kayla and Brittany among the people who had gathered to watch, but I wasn't really in the mood to deal with Brittany's PMS attitude or whatever was going on with her. I wasn't even in the mood to hear about how disgustingly happy Kayla was now that she and Lucas had found each other. I was glad for her, but maybe I was also a little jealous that she had no doubts whatsoever about her feelings toward Lucas, while uncertainty about my feelings toward Connor had begun to plague me.

I leaned against a tree, relishing its sturdiness. I'm all about nature; I appreciate every aspect of it, and I draw comfort from it. I needed a little comfort just then. As I looked around, I realized sadly that Connor was right. There wasn't as much laughter as usual. Everyone seemed to realize that our world was on the brink of shifting— and we just weren't comfortable with aspects of shifting that weren't directly related to our bodies. Maybe that was the reason we still used terms like *mate* and only the guys publicly declared their intended. We were archaic in a quaint sort of way.

As it grew dark, a few torches were lit for the benefit of those of us who hadn't had our first transformations yet. Those who could shift had the keen night vision of a wolf, even when they weren't in wolf form. After the initial transformation, we brought many of our enhanced abilities back to our human shape. On one hand, I couldn't wait. And on another, I was still terrified. What would it really be like? And what if I'd made a mistake in selecting my mate?

"So who's ahead?"

My heart galloped at the familiar raspy voice so near my ear. I don't know anyone else who moves as silently as Rafe. Glancing back over my shoulder, hoping he didn't hear the wild pounding of my heart, I smiled casually at him. "The sons, I think. How come you're not playing?"

An odd expression crossed his face—and I remembered that his dad had died. "I'm sorry. That was thoughtless—"

"No big deal. It's not like it was any great loss to the clan."

"But it was to you."

"Not really. So is this the dullest summer solstice celebration we've ever had, or have I just outgrown them?"

It was obvious that he wanted to change the subject. His dad had died in a car crash that he'd caused after getting behind the wheel drunk. I accepted the new topic with grace. "Oh, it's definitely the dullest."

"You want to sneak away for a while? I've got my bike."

I felt a spark of pleasure that he'd asked, and abruptly realized how inappropriate my reaction was. "Thanks, but I can't."

Because I couldn't get that dream out of my mind, or

the way he'd watched me during the meeting. And if we were alone, out in the woods . . .

The truth was that I didn't trust myself. Would I give into temptation? Rafe called to some part of me, something inside me that I didn't understand. He made me think about getting up close and personal with him—and Connor had already claimed that privilege with me.

I looked back toward the game, watched as Connor raced out and caught the pass thrown by Lucas. Only a few people cheered. It was as though everyone wanted to make sure that no one in the forest heard us—as though we'd reverted back to being ultrasecret. The way we were acting, we might as well have been afraid of our own shadows.

"You know they'll play for a couple more hours," Rafe said. "We're legendary for our stamina. Even the old guys are like Energizer bunnies: They just keep on going and going."

"I know, but—"

"Come on, Lindsey. I'm just talking about a ride on my bike. It's way more fun than leaning against a tree."

And here I'd always thought he was a guy of few words.

But he was right. I was bored out of my mind. Rafe and I were friends. I could go with him and not do anything to betray Connor. Couldn't I? Sure I could. I never wanted to hurt Connor. It was one of the reasons that I was keeping buried so many of my doubts about us. "Connor and I—"

"I know," he said with a hint of wistfulness. "You're destined for each other. He's got your name inked on his shoulder and everything."

I narrowed my eyes at him. "You have a tattoo. Whose name is it?"

Usually a guy declared his mate before he had a symbol representing her name etched on his skin, but Rafe wasn't about following rules. Only recently had we learned that he had a tattoo.

"Come with me," he dared. "Maybe I'll tell you."

"I'm not going to do anything Connor wouldn't like."

"I won't ask you to."

His voice held a resignation that I didn't quite understand. It made me wonder again if he felt the same pull toward me that I did toward him. Besides, I couldn't deny that I was curious about his ink.

"I can't stay away long," I said quietly. When the game ended, Connor would be looking for me. I didn't want to give him any reason to question my loyalty. And the more time I spent with Rafe, the greater the chance of me doing something I shouldn't. Like finding out if his kisses in reality were as amazing as the one in my dream.

"Just a quick ride. No one will even miss us," he promised.

I glanced back at him and nodded. It was easier to do things I wasn't supposed to if I didn't actually give voice to them.

THREE

As the wind whipped my white-blond hair, which flowed like silk behind me, I felt carefree, unburdened by the future. I tightened my arms around Rafe and pressed my cheek against his strong, broad back. His headlights remained off. I knew it was probably crazy, but I trusted him not to get us killed as he sped through the dark forest on his motorbike. Even for a Shifter, he has excellent night vision.

I laughed just for the hell of it, simply because I could do so with no one but Rafe to hear me, and the sound reverberated between the trees, echoing off the thick canopy of leaves overhead. Rafe's booming laugh drowned out mine. It was so wonderful to hear joyous laughter again. I hated that Bio-Chrome had taken it away from us, had turned our celebration into a wake.

Rafe and I had grown up in Tarrant, a small town near the entrance to the national forest. Although he's two years older than me, we'd gone to the same schools. We'd even been in a couple of the same classes. I was an academic whiz; he wasn't particularly. What was advanced for me was normal for him. I'm into using my brain, while he's all about using his hands.

A shiver coursed through me as I remembered the dream—the way his large hands had caressed my back and held me close.

Among the guys, Rafe is known for what he can do with mechanics, with a motor. Evidence of his skill was purring beneath me now as we raced over ground where there was no actual trail. It was a prototype he was working on: a two-wheeler all-terrain vehicle that could cut a neat swath through the forest without struggling over rugged ground. He's a mechanical genius.

He cut a curve around a tree, and we leaned into it. I squeezed him tighter, refusing to scream, but my heart was galloping. It was a real rush. He laughed again, and I knew it was because he lives for danger. He isn't afraid of anything.

He swung the bike around and skidded to a stop at

the edge of a cliff that would have scared the hell out of me if I'd seen it coming—but with my face pressed to his back, all I'd seen were the tall trees rushing by.

He turned off the engine and everything went quiet. I needed to pop my ears, so I slid off the back of the bike, not expecting my legs to feel like jelly after the ride. I stumbled back and almost fell but came to an abrupt halt when Rafe grabbed my arm. I hadn't seen him move. That, too, was a result of the initial change: a swiftness that was beyond human. Bringing his arms around me, he tucked me in against his chest, supporting me. I knew I should have pushed him back, should have welcomed falling to the ground. I knew standing so near to him was wrong, but he felt so good, so strong. Why did this feel so different from when Connor held me? Connor was a Dark Guardian. He wasn't someone to be messed with. But I felt so safe with Rafe holding me, as though nothing could ever hurt me.

"Just give your legs a minute to adjust," Rafe said quietly, and I heard him inhaling my scent. Smell is one of a Shifter's most powerful senses. We aren't into perfumes or artificial fragrances. Pheromones, the very essence of a person, appeal to us.

"Why aren't your legs unsteady?" I asked, wondering why I sounded breathless when I hadn't been running. Being near him made it difficult to breathe, no doubt adding to my sudden embarrassing inability to stay upright.

"Because I'm used to riding."

I could smell his earthy scent. It was richer, more powerful than anything that could be bought in a store. He was wearing a T-shirt that clung to him like a second skin, and I could feel the comforting warmth of his body seeping through it. Even though today the sun had warmed Earth longer than on any other day of the year, here in the forest near the Canadian border, the night was cool.

I wanted to stay nestled against him all night, but there were too many reasons why I shouldn't. Or maybe there was just one powerful reason: Connor. I could never cheat on him, and I fought to convince myself that being here with Rafe now wasn't a betrayal. I hadn't done anything to be ashamed of. Where was the harm in simply riding a bike, even if it was with a hot guy who had visited my dream last night? I couldn't control my dreams, could I?

"I'm okay now," I said, pushing against him just a little.

I felt his reluctance to let me go as his arms slowly eased away from me. Suddenly I feared that I was on far more dangerous ground than I'd realized. Maybe to Rafe I wasn't just a convenient solution to a boring night.

Skirting around him, I walked carefully and slowly to the edge of the cliff, testing the ground with my toe to make sure it was firm before I gave it my full weight. I'd grown up near these woods. They'd been my playground. I was comfortable in them. Looking down, I saw only the black abyss, but I knew trees and shrubbery followed the steep slope down into a valley. Only the stars served to delineate the ground from the night sky, which was so vast that I felt incredibly small.

On silent feet, Rafe came to stand beside me. "Guess it's too late to make a wish on the first star," he said quietly, but his deep voice still carried on the light breeze that was stirring my hair.

"The first one came out hours ago."

"Which one do you think it was?"

Rafe was a warrior, a protector, a Dark Guardian. He didn't strike me as someone who believed in the whimsy of wishing on stars. But still, I pointed upward. "That one right there, near the tail of the Big Dipper."

"That'll do. I wish—"

Quickly, I pressed my fingertips to his warm lips. "If you say it aloud, it won't come true."

"Since it involves you, it won't come true anyway, unless *you* know what it is."

Not for the first time, I regretted leaving the festivities, regretted that I'd put myself in this position. I loved to be adventuresome, but I was moving out of my comfort zone now. We were traveling into unexplored territory that was both thrilling and terrifying.

"You shouldn't say anything that you might regret," I warned him.

"I spend a lot of time thinking about kissing you."

Not exactly what I wanted to hear. Oh, who am I kidding? Every girl wants to believe that a great guy thinks about kissing her. The problem was that now I knew I had to deal with it.

"You shouldn't," I insisted sternly, trying to stay in control of this situation when I felt it slipping away from me.

"I shouldn't want you for my mate either, but I do."

The shock of his somber confession left me lightheaded. Yes, we'd stared at each other from time to time, but he'd never truly indicated that he saw me as anything other than part of the pack. I felt as though the ground was shifting beneath me.

"What about the girl whose name is tattooed on your shoulder?" The Celtic symbol is always intricate and unreadable, decipherable only by the male until he shares it with the female.

"God, Lindsey, you have to know by now. . . ."

I felt as though all the air had been sucked right out of me. "It's my name? Why would you do that? You knew Connor and I . . . that we were . . . why would you choose me?"

"Because you're the one I want."

His voice held such surety—no doubts whatsoever. How could he be so convinced?

"You don't . . . you can't mean it. Come on, Rafe, you know I'm with Connor."

"Why? Because you've always been with him? What if he's not the right one? What if he's not your true mate?"

It made me angry to hear him voice the doubts I'd been having lately. "That's not fair, Rafe. Why tell me this now? Why not last year before Connor declared me as his mate?"

"Because I didn't know last year that I would feel this way. The first time I saw you after I came back from college I felt as though a tree had fallen on me. I've tried to fight this . . . attraction. You have to believe that. But it's just growing stronger."

I was unsettled. I couldn't think. I didn't know what to say.

Into the silence, he asked, "Do you ever think about kissing me?"

The dream roared into my head. Obviously my subconscious had given some thought to kissing him, but I wasn't about to admit that.

"I'm with Connor," I repeated sternly. I had been with

him since I turned sixteen. He was like the old robe that you wore even after it got all frayed and ratty, because it had molded itself through the years until it was perfect for you.

"That's not an answer," Rafe insisted.

"It wouldn't be fair to Connor." That was as close as I was going to come to admitting that, at the moment, I wanted nothing as much as I wanted to kiss Rafe.

He sighed deeply. "Why couldn't Connor be a jerk? It'd make things a lot easier. I could just challenge him—"

"Don't you dare!" Suddenly I was almost shouting, about to go into panic mode. We were human, but we were also beast, and in our world a challenge wasn't made lightly. A challenge was a fight to the death.

"So you do care about him," he said as though he was surprised by the revelation.

"Of course I care about him."

"But do you love him?"

I knew I was supposed to respond with a resounding *yes*, but my doubts surfaced once again. I did love Connor, but was my love for him deep enough?

I peered over at Rafe, who was staring up at the sky as though he'd find my answer there. The little bit of crescent moon and starlight limned his profile, revealing the strong jut of his chin, the sharp blade of his nose. His silhouette was powerful, as powerful as he was. He'd always seemed older, stronger than the others. Maybe because he'd worked in his dad's auto shop when he wasn't a sherpa. Late at night, he still did so. I often saw the light on in that old shed when I drove by. Sometimes I thought about stopping, but just like now, I knew it would be a bad idea. So why had I agreed to go on this ride with him? To quell my adventuresome spirit? For a last chance to do something I wasn't supposed to do?

Our kind work in the outside world just like humans do. My dad is a lawyer; so is Connor's. They share a very successful practice. I've never gone without; I've always had anything I wanted. Rafe, on the other hand, must have always wanted things he couldn't have, things he'd never been able to afford. Was he suddenly interested in me because I was unattainable?

Instead of answering his question, I posed a scenario of my own. "Maybe you just want me because you can't have me. Forbidden things are always sweeter, right?"

He turned around to face me squarely. "You really think that's what this is?"

"I don't know. Maybe."

"Easy enough to find out. . . . Kiss me," he challenged. "If that's all it is, one kiss should satisfy this hunger I have for you."

"Hunger? You make it sound like you're going to devour me."

"That doesn't even begin to describe what I'm feeling, Lindsey. It's primal. It's like my wolf prowling inside me, waiting for yours to emerge."

"So it's just the wolves?"

"You can't separate them. It's not two different beings. I'm the wolf. And I'm the human. I think about you all the time, think about kissing you—I want to be with you during your first full moon."

The intensity of his words terrified me. Connor was fun. He laughed and teased. Rafe was all serious, dark, and foreboding.

I moved around to face him.

The ground beneath my feet suddenly crumbled. I shrieked, my arms flailing as I felt myself dropping. Rafe grabbed me, but I had fallen too far away already. He couldn't pull me to safety.

All he could do was wrap himself around me as we both tumbled into the black abyss.

FOUR

Much to my astonishment, the landing wasn't nearly as painful as I'd expected. I only had the wind knocked out of me. Rafe had somehow managed to twist around so he cushioned my landing. I was straddling him. One of his arms held me close. My face was buried in the curve of his neck, and his wonderful scent filled my nostrils.

Lying incredibly still, he gave a low groan.

"Are you okay?" I asked.

"Yeah."

It sounded as though he'd forced out the word, and I realized that with me on top of him, he was probably having difficulty breathing. I knew I should have rolled off him. Instead I stayed where I was, relishing the firmness of his body beneath me when I knew I shouldn't. If he turned his head just a little and I lifted mine a fraction, our mouths would meet and . . .

"You shouldn't have said everything that you said up there, Rafe," I whispered. I should have been scolding him, but my words came out more wistful than forceful.

"I thought you should know."

"It's too late."

"No, it's not," he said vehemently. "Not until the full moon."

I couldn't do that to Connor, and whatever it was that I was feeling toward Rafe—well, maybe it was just temporary insanity.

"I've seen you watching me," he said quietly. "I thought maybe you were feeling the way I feel."

"Honestly, Rafe? I don't know what I'm feeling." Other than scared, and I wasn't going to admit that.

I scrambled up and crouched beside him. It was so very dark down there, but I heard movement, so I knew Rafe had sat up. He moaned again.

"Are you sure you're okay?" I asked.

"Okay enough."

What did that mean? But he sounded petulant, so I didn't pursue it. His ego had to be bruised. I wanted to tell him about my dream, tell him that I had been noticing and thinking about him lately, but that confession would only make things worse, and it would be harder on us both. It was best that we just forget this night ever happened. And the best way to achieve that end was to get back to Wolford before anyone noticed.

"So how are we going to get out of here?" I asked.

"I can see. I'll lead the way."

I stood up. He took my hand and guided it to his back.

"Hang onto my belt, so it's easier to follow me."

"Wouldn't it be easier if you shifted into a wolf?"

"Not until I can get you to where there's some light—you can use the headlight on my bike."

"You're not making any sense."

"Lindsey, I landed at a bad angle. I think I broke my arm."

"Oh my God, Rafe! Why didn't you say that before?"

"Because it wouldn't change anything, and I didn't want you to worry."

"God. Sometimes you are such a . . . guy."

He actually chuckled, while I wanted to shriek. Now I understood the strain in his voice. He was fighting the pain. I didn't know whether to have an *aw-isn't-that-sweet-for-not-wanting-to-worry-me* moment or a *how-stupid-can-you-get-you-obviously-need-help* moment, because he was trying to protect me in a strange kind of way. I settled for keeping my voice even when I asked, "How bad?"

"Bad enough that you're going to have to hold it together for a little while after I shift so it can mend straight."

One of the perks of being able to shift was rapid cell rejuvenation. Unless we received a fatal head or heart wound or the weapon that struck us was silver, we had the ability to heal quickly.

"We should take care of it before we try to scale back up to the top," I told him.

"You're not going to be able to see."

Probably a good thing since he'd have to remove his clothes to shift.

"I've got touch. Which arm?"

"Left."

Great. I knew he was left-handed. So he was going to try to get us back to the top with one good arm, and it wasn't his strongest. Because he'd already moved my hand to his belt, I was at a good starting point. I tugged his T-shirt out of his jeans, then very carefully skimmed my hands across his back, over his shoulder, down his arm—

"Oh my God, Rafe!" I cried when my hand encountered a hard edge that had to be bone. He inhaled a sharp breath. I could smell the metallic scent of blood now and felt the warmth of it coating my fingers. His bone had

46

lacerated the skin. "You *think* it might be broken?"

"I didn't want to worry you," he repeated.

Tears stung my eyes. He had to be hurting. As gently as I could, I maneuvered his T-shirt over his head while he bit back a groan. For the first time in several weeks, I found myself wishing for a full moon so I could see more clearly. The sliver of moon and a few stars scattered across the night sky were pretty useless. And it didn't help that we were at the base of the cliff, with brush and trees all around us.

Once the T-shirt was free, he said, "I can take care of the rest. Just sit there and when I come over, you'll have to search for the break and push the two pieces of bone back together."

"Okay." Still clutching his T-shirt, I dropped down to the ground and tucked my legs beneath me. So much for our plan to sneak away for just a little while. We'd probably already be heading back if I'd just let him kiss me.

I heard the brush rustle as Rafe shucked off his boots and jeans. I refused to envision him naked and shifting into wolf form. The shift would happen in the blink of an eye, faster than I could imagine it.

I barely made out his silhouette as he limped toward me, in wolf form now. I was glad there wasn't enough moonlight to allow me to see the pain in his eyes. He rested his head in my lap. Very gently, I buried my fingers

47

in his fur and followed the line of his shoulder until I reached his left foreleg.

"I know this is going to hurt, and I'm so sorry," I said as I struggled and snapped the broken bone back into place. He stiffened, but made no sound. Even in wolf form, he had to be macho. "It'll be okay now." I released a self-conscious laugh. "I don't know why I'm talking to you. You can read my mind, right? I wish I could read yours. Or maybe not. Yours is probably filled with pain right now."

When we shift, we become telepathic. It's how we communicate with others while in wolf form. As a bonus, we can also read the minds of those who aren't in wolf form.

Rafe licked my forearm, maybe to stop my babbling or just to let me know that he was okay. I wanted to bury my face in his fur and weep. I hated that he was going through this. I felt helpless. There was little I could do. He licked me again.

"Not fair," I said. "Don't think I don't know that's a wolf's version of a kiss." I tried to blank my mind so he wouldn't know how much I enjoyed having him this close to me, even if it was in animal form. I became aware that there was no more flowing blood. I dared to skim my thumb over what had been torn flesh. It was smooth now, healed. The muscle and bone would probably take longer.

Our healing abilities were one of the reasons that Bio-Chrome was interested in us. But I didn't want to think about that. Even as I tried to empty all my thoughts, I couldn't help but think about how beautiful Rafe was as a wolf. I'd seen him in wolf form before, so even with the low moonlight, I knew what he looked like. His fur was as black as his hair, so black that at certain angles it appeared a deep blue. It was gorgeous, the most gorgeous fur I'd ever seen.

Lucas's coat was a combination of black, white, silver, and brown. Connor, with his sandy-blond hair, was more of a golden color. My hair was a pale blond that was almost white. I wondered how I'd look as a wolf. Would I resemble the white Arctic wolf? Would I be pretty? Or would there be nothing special about me?

It was bad enough to worry about my hair, makeup, and clothes, to always want to look attractive, but now to start worrying about my appearance as a wolf. . . .

Rafe nuzzled my arm, and I realized that he was letting me know that I didn't have to hold onto his front leg any longer. I stroked his neck and shoulder, relishing the sensation of his fur touching my fingers. "I know healing, not to mention shifting, can be tiring. Just rest for a bit."

I guessed I was talking aloud out of habit.

You're beautiful, I thought. It was something I'd never say out loud. Just like I'd never tell him that I thought he

49

was good looking—sexy, to be precise—in human form.

My thoughts were traveling where they shouldn't. I started silently humming a Nine Inch Nails song, trying to fill my mind with a chaotic beat that drowned out anything else.

Rafe moved away from me. I immediately missed his warmth and the feel of my fingers brushing over his fur. I wanted to call him back. Instead, I started humming aloud.

Something landed in my lap.

"My clothes. Bundle them up." He'd shifted back to human form to speak to me, to let me know that his arm had healed. "Then grab onto my fur. I'm stronger, more surefooted as a wolf."

By the time I'd finished bundling up his clothes and tucking them beneath one arm, he'd shifted again and was nuzzling my leg. I grabbed a mass of his fur and let him lead me. It was slow going as he searched for outcroppings that I could use as steps. I lost my footing once or twice and slipped back a little, but he was always there, nudging me with his snout, insisting wordlessly that I try again.

Eventually we made it back up to the cliff. I dropped his clothes as soon as I was over the edge of the cliff. I wandered over to the motorbike; I knew he was shifting and getting dressed behind me. I tried not to think about what he looked like with his clothes off.

"So, hey, thanks for your help with the broken bone."

I startled, laughed, and turned around. "I'm always surprised by how quiet you can be."

"It's our nature to be stealthy. Never sure where a predator might strike." I could feel his gaze on me. "I guess you don't want to put my kiss theory to the test before we head back."

More than I dared to admit. "No. It's a really bad idea."

"Depends on your point of view, I guess." Moving past me, he straddled the bike and turned on the motor. He also flicked on the lights this time. "Climb on. We'd better get back before we're missed."

I was afraid it might be a little late for that. I scrambled onto the bike, pressed up against him, and wrapped my arms securely around his waist.

He turned his head to the side. "Lindsey?"

"Yeah?"

"I think you're beautiful, too."

He kicked the side stand, revved the engine, and took off before I could respond. It was a good thing, because I had no idea what to say. But all the way back to the home of our elders, I hummed a happy tune in my head.

FIVE

When we got back to Wolford, Rafe swiped an electronic keycard at the gate to open it. It was a recent addition to our defenses, evidence of our strange place in the world, between the archaic and the modern.

He puttered over to an area where a few jeeps and all-terrain vehicles were parked. It was late. The festivities had ended. Everything was quiet as we walked toward the large mansion.

"You go on in," Rafe said, coming to a stop. "We don't want to be seen together."

"Right." It would be a disaster to run into Connor now. How could I even begin to explain? I couldn't. "Uh, listen, thanks for getting me away from all the doom and gloom for awhile."

"Almost getting you killed was a great substitute."

I smiled. "That was my fault, totally. I've hiked in these woods often enough to know that I shouldn't stand at the very edge of a cliff," I said, although I still felt as though I were standing at the edge of one. Metaphorically, anyway. "Have you ever considered Brittany? You know, for a mate? She's available."

He released a harsh laugh. "*What* are you doing?"

"Trying to offer alternatives," I said sincerely.

"I don't want alternatives. I don't feel the same hunger around Brittany. I don't feel anything for her other than mild curiosity and light-hearted friendship. I don't wonder what it would be like to kiss her. I don't feel a need to lay with my body curled around hers. I don't"—he leaned in and skimmed his lips along the side of my face, inhaling as he went, causing heat to swirl through me—"I don't relish her scent. I don't dream about her. I want *you*."

Before I could respond, he'd turned on his heel and started walking away. My heart was beating erratically and my mouth had gone dry. He'd said it as though he wasn't giving up. I didn't know whether to feel flattered or worried.

I almost chased after him. I had to try to talk some

sense into him. Instead I let him go, refusing to acknowledge that a small part of me was glad he'd rejected the notion of being with Brittany. Was I a total mess or what?

Inside the residence, a few lights were on low, but it was still amazingly quiet. I assumed everyone was in bed. I headed for the stairs.

"Lindsey?"

My heart almost stopped at the sound of Connor's voice. I turned slowly to see him standing in the doorway of the parlor. I swallowed hard before saying, "Hey."

He walked toward me. "Where'd you disappear to? I couldn't find you."

I shrugged. "I just . . . everyone was so melancholy and worried that I just wanted to be by myself for awhile."

He studied me with his deep-blue eyes, and for a moment he looked sad. My heart nearly stammered to a stop. I wanted to apologize for going off with Rafe, but I was afraid it would only worsen things. I truly didn't want to hurt Connor. And the truth absolutely would hurt him. Finally he nodded. "So, listen, the sherpas are going to head back to the park entrance in the morning so we can be back in time to guide that scout troop that's hired us. Thought we'd catch a ride with Lucas. He came in his jeep."

"I'll be ready."

"Okay. See you then."

I knew I should say something more, but guilt was gnawing at me. I hurried up the stairs and down the long hallway, passing various closed doors. Turning a corner, I came up short at the sight of Kayla and Lucas intertwined like a pretzel, kissing in front of the window, limned by the faint moonlight. Judging by the heat they were generating, I was surprised the window hadn't fogged up. They were so lost in each other that they hadn't heard me.

As quietly as possible I slipped back around the corner, dropped into a crouch, and pressed my back up against the wall. I had an insane urge to weep. I hardly ever cried, but suddenly I felt lost and so incredibly lonely.

Why hadn't Connor and I sneaked away to a corner for a quick lip-lock? Or a long one, for that matter? Where was our passion? Would it come after my transformation? Would we be unable to keep our hands off each other then?

I thought about Rafe and how I'd wanted him to hold me, to touch me, to kiss me and how hard it had been to step away from him when I'd wanted to rush toward him. But that was just lust, right? Merely a physical reaction. Love was more than that. Love was internal. Love was your heart and your soul. It was everything that was important. It was—

My thoughts came to a screeching halt as Lucas came

around the corner and nearly tripped over me. "Whoa! Lindsey, sorry!"

"Get a room next time, why don't you?" I teased as I shot to my feet.

He released a little groan of embarrassment for getting caught in a passionate embrace. If not for the shadows in the hallway, I might even have seen him blushing. He'd always been the most private guy I'd known. I'd had no idea that he was interested in Kayla until they were a bonded couple.

I was acutely aware of him studying me intently. He could perform a third-degree interrogation without words. I wasn't in the mood for it. "Good night," I said.

Before I'd taken my first step, though, he grabbed my arm. "Are you okay? You seem . . . distracted."

How would he react if I confessed that I doubted my feelings for Connor? Since he was friends with both Rafe and Connor, would it put him in an awkward position? I figured the fewer people who knew, the better.

"I just stumbled across an R-rated encounter. I was trying not to visualize it. And now I'm going to bed."

To my immense relief, he let me go. As our pack leader, he felt like he had to watch out for all of us, but I didn't think he could help me with my problem.

I went into the room I shared with Kayla and Brittany. Kayla was sitting on her bed. Stretched out on a mat, Brittany was doing sit-ups. Judging by the sweat on her brow, I figured she was nearing her nightly one hundred. Me? I preferred to curl up with a good book.

"Where have *you* been?" Brittany asked, her breaths coming in short little puffs as she kept up her tempo.

"Where do you think? With Connor."

"So what were you, the invisible sherpa? Because he was looking for you."

I dropped down onto my bed and toed off my sneakers. "I just wanted to be alone."

She stopped exercising and began stretching. "So why not just say that?"

Guilt. "Maybe I don't like getting the third degree."

"It was only one question."

Trying to work out the tension, I rolled my shoulders. "Sorry. This Bio-Chrome mess just has me on edge." I glanced over at Kayla, who was now dragging her brush through her long, red hair. "Usually the summer solstice celebration is a little more festive."

"I actually had a great time," she said brightly. "I got to talk to all these people who knew my parents. My adoptive parents are awesome and all, but before this summer, I never felt as though I truly belonged anywhere, you know? But here, I just feel like I've come home."

Kayla's parents had been killed when she was younger, and she'd been adopted by a non-Shifter family.

Until this summer, she hadn't even realized that our kind existed. Talk about blowing apart your concept of reality. I couldn't even imagine the shock of it.

Grabbing my backpack from the foot of the bed, I scrounged around until I found cotton shorts and a tank top to sleep in. Once I'd changed clothes, I sat cross-legged on my bed. Brittany had finished her exercises and was getting ready for bed. I figured it was time for a little intimate girl talk. "Listen, Kayla . . . the guys will never talk about what it's like when they shift. They're all secretive about it. What was it really like? The first time?"

"Oh, gosh, it's hard to explain." With her back pressed against the headboard, she closed her eyes and intertwined her fingers together. "It's so intense. It's as if pleasure and pain are all mixed up, and you don't know what you should really be feeling, and then all of a sudden—*bam!* It's maximum overload and suddenly you're body is shaped differently and your mind is more . . . aware." Smiling softly, she opened her eyes. "It's awesome."

"I've heard it's excruciatingly painful," Brittany said.

Kayla nodded. "It is—if you go through it alone. Like the guys have to, but when Lucas was with me, he kept me distracted, so the pain was just an irritant."

"Do you think it would have been more painful if you didn't love him?" I asked.

"I wouldn't want to go through it with someone I didn't love. It's really kinda personal and private."

Not exactly what I wanted to hear. I did love Connor, but was it enough? I mean desperately, *my-life-would-be-over-if-he-didn't-love-me-back* love him?

"Sounds like I'm screwed," Brittany said. "I either go through it alone—and maybe die in the process—or I go through something intimate with someone I don't love, which sounds icky and worse than going through it alone."

"Someone will claim you, Brittany," I insisted.

"I only have two weeks! My time is running out. Besides, I don't want just anyone. I want someone who looks at me the way Lucas looks at Kayla, like she's the moon and the stars."

Kayla laughed lightly. "Does Lucas really look at me like that?"

"Oh, God, does he ever," I said. It had been strange to see strong, silent Lucas fall so hard. But like all girls, I craved a guy who thought *I* was his destiny. It was both terrifying and romantic. In most societies, girls our age aren't supposed to fall in love so young, but we aren't most societies. Ours is ruled by destiny.

"Of course, you look at him the same way," I told her.

She grinned brightly. "I probably do. I'm so nuts about him."

"So maybe your true mate just hasn't noticed you yet, Brittany," I said, trying to be positive. In truth, it was really rare for a girl to be approaching her time for change without a guy speaking up for her.

"Yeah, right. And he's just going to stumble into me sometime during the next two weeks? Get real. I'm going to sleep," Brittany said, just before she reached out and turned off the lamp by her bed, immersing us in the darkness.

I felt so bad for her, but I also realized that she didn't want my pity. She was always trying to prove how strong she was.

I was too restless to slip beneath the covers and try to go to sleep. I was afraid that another dream like the one I'd had the night before was waiting for me. I walked over to the window and peered between the curtains. For some reason, all that talk about finding one's true mate, about going through the first transformation with someone you truly loved . . . it had left me feeling hollow and confused. I would go through it with Connor. Why wasn't I comforted by that realization?

I heard the light padding of bare feet.

"Are you okay?" Kayla whispered as she came to stand beside me.

"Yeah," I said, my voice equally low. It usually didn't take Brittany long to fall asleep, but I didn't want to risk disturbing her. She wouldn't appreciate my confusion, wouldn't offer me solace. Kayla would.

"You know . . . one thing that happens after that first transformation is that all your senses are heightened," Kayla said softly.

"Yeah, I've heard." I wondered what she was getting at. Unlike Kayla, all this wasn't new to me. My parents were Shifters. I'd grown up around Shifters.

"Scent is the one I notice the most. You know how you go into your favorite restaurant and it just smells so good?"

"Sure."

"Well, now it's as though I can smell each individual scent. I don't smell lasagna. I smell tomato and garlic and noodles and mozzarella. I smell each distinct ingredient. When I go into a room filled with people, I smell each person. Like right now. I can smell a hint of Connor . . . and a whole lot of Rafe."

Busted!

"Are you trying to make a point?" I asked, irritated with her sense of smell and slightly panicked at the thought that maybe Connor had smelled Rafe on me, too. Maybe that was the reason he'd seemed distant and hadn't pulled me into the corner for a kiss.

"You were with Rafe a lot more than you were with Connor tonight. It's not any of my business, but if you need to talk"—she touched my shoulder, squeezed—"you're my best friend. I'm here for you."

"I don't know, Kayla. I don't know what I'm feeling right now. I know when you have your first transformation that you bond with the guy—"

"I think the bond needs to be there first, Lindsey. Yes, it'll grow deeper after what you go through, but the emotions need an anchor."

"Connor's a good guy. He's always steady. I can depend on him." But did that mean what we felt for each other was right, was as deep as it might be? If I told him I had doubts, would I lose his friendship? Could I stand to lose it after having it for most of my life?

"But do you love him?" Kayla asked.

Why did that question seem to be a common theme tonight? And why in the hell didn't I know the answer?

The next morning I caught up with my mom and dad for breakfast. The dining room had lots of small, cloth-covered round tables so families could engage in intimate conversations. What I got, though, was the third degree.

"We didn't see you last night," Dad said conversationally, but I knew a lawyer tactic when I heard one. His dark hair was turning silver at the temples. It made him appear very distinguished, even with his brown eyes homing in on me as if he were a wolf scenting a rabbit.

"I was hanging around with my friends, as usual."

"Connor was looking for you," Mom said. Even in

the wilderness, my mom looked as though she could take tea with the queen. Yes, my family—just like Connor's—was among the elite of our clan. We never got our hands dirty from making an engine work; we hired people for that sort of thing. We'd even hired Rafe's dad, until he'd declined into heavy drinking and become undependable and quarrelsome.

"He found me," I assured her.

"I'm not sure why he would have to look for you in the first place," Mom said, tucking a stray strand of her blond hair back into the French twist she wore.

"I got bored watching the football game, so I walked around for a while."

"Do you know that when a person lies the scent of their skin changes?" Dad asked, casually buttering his toast.

I groaned inwardly. *It's impossible to keep a secret around here.* I decided to change the subject.

"Is that why you're so successful in court? Because you know when the witness is lying?"

"That's one of the reasons. So do you want to try another answer?"

"No. I'm happy with the one I gave."

He narrowed his eyes at me. That predatory look was probably another reason he was so successful. If I hadn't grown up with it, I'd be shaking in my sneakers.

I knew he was more growl than bite—well, except when he was in wolf form. Then he could rip out a throat without remorse. It was rumored that he'd actually done it once—to a guy who had killed a couple of teens and gotten off on a technicality. But if that was true, Dad had never admitted it. He believed in the law of the jungle, but he was all about working within the confines of the Static law.

"I saw you with that Lowell boy last night," he said with deadly calm.

I felt anger rising up within me.

"Boy? Rafe is a Dark Guardian, protecting your butt—"

"Watch your tone with me, young lady."

Sometimes my parents could be so . . . well, parenty. It was irritating. "Why didn't you just ask about him to begin with, instead of treating me like I'm a bad guy on a witness stand?"

The muscle in my dad's cheek jerked. "Trust me, sweetheart, I'm a little more ruthless with the bad guys. You don't want to go there."

"We're just worried, honey," Mom said, restoring tranquility to the table. She was good at that. She owned a world-class spa in our small town. It drew practically as many tourists as the forest did. "I've been where you are. I know sometimes things can get scary when you're approaching your time, but you have Connor. And he's better suited to you."

Better suited? I thought about Brittany's shoe comment the day before. It did sound like my parents and I were selecting accessories. It was kind of insulting, to both Connor and me.

"Meaning . . . ?" I prompted.

"Connor comes from the same type of background as you do. Rafe's family is a little more . . . coarse."

"His dad was a drunk, but he's not."

"Rafe was arrested for stealing a car," Dad said.

He'd hotwired a car a few years back—I'd forgotten about that. "When he was sixteen. Right after his dad died in that awful car accident. Maybe he was acting out. He hasn't done anything wrong since."

"You mean he hasn't been *caught* doing anything wrong."

"Okay, look. Rafe is my friend. He's Connor's friend. If you're going to put him down, I'm out of here."

"Were you with him last night?" Mom asked.

"Nothing happened." I knew that's what they were really asking. Was I cheating on my boyfriend? On the perfect Connor? I scooted my chair back. "I've got to head out with the others. It was great seeing you both." *Not. Never was.* They wanted me to be what they were: rich, successful, sure of themselves.

Before I could stomp off, Mom reached out and gave me a quick hug; we barely touched. I'd heard some Shifter families actually roll around on the floor together like wolf cubs. Not my parents. Sometimes I wondered if they weren't quite comfortable with the animalistic side of our legacy.

Dad said, "Do you need any money?" It was his equivalent of *I love you*.

"No, I'm good. Getting a paycheck every week." I hugged him because I knew other families might be watching. Our family motto was never to let on if anything was wrong. Dad was probably going to run for governor someday. Nothing about us was supposed to create scandal. That was probably the reason that they were more comfortable with Connor than with Rafe. Connor was an Eagle Scout. Rafe had spent time in juvie.

I picked up my backpack and headed outside, quickly sweeping my gaze over the parking area. Rafe's bike was gone. I figured he'd already headed out.

Connor was standing at the bottom of the steps, staring out into the wilderness.

"Spare me from another breakfast with my parents," I grumbled as I joined him.

"Tell me about it. Dad and I got into an argument," he said wearily.

"About what?"

"Nothing you should worry about."

But shouldn't we share tough moments like this?

"I didn't see you in the dining room," I said.

He gave me an ironic grin. "Met with them early. The elders had a special meeting with some of us afterward."

"I didn't hear about that."

He shrugged. "It was just the guys."

Brittany was so right. We're such a sexist group. I couldn't keep the irritation out of my voice. "What are you guys doing? Planning some secretive operation that's too dangerous for the girls to be involved in?"

"It's secretive, but only dangerous if Brittany finds out."

"She's not the only one who'll be pissed off for not being included."

"It's not what you think."

"Then what is it?" I prodded.

He shifted his gaze back to whatever he'd been staring at before I joined him. "Connor? What's going on?"

"You have to promise not to tell."

That sounded so childish, but whatever. I wanted to know what was going on. "It goes without saying."

"Still, say it."

"I promise not to tell." It was so unlike him to be melodramatic that I was starting to get a little worried.

"The elders are concerned about Brittany. You know.

Because she doesn't have a mate. They were looking for a volunteer."

I was appalled that they'd tried to hook her up with someone who didn't love her. Especially after what Kayla had confessed, about how intimate shifting with someone truly was. And Connor was right to keep it to himself. Brittany would explode if she found out.

"What? You mean like . . . a pity mate?"

He looked really uncomfortable, and I realized that was exactly what this was. Worse than a blind date. She might as well sign up for an arranged marriage.

"Connor, this is insane!" Then I had another thought. Maybe one of the guys did have an interest in her but was too shy to come forward. If his hand was forced . . .

"Did someone volunteer?" I asked.

"No. They drew a name."

"This is totally nuts."

"Look, she doesn't have to *choose* him. But he's going to be part of our sherpa team, hang with us, determine if there's any chemistry there."

Oh, there would definitely be chemistry—like an explosion in a lab—if Brittany discovered that the elders were trying to set her up. On the other hand, we didn't get a lot of time to hang out with the other Dark Guardians, so maybe it was simply that she hadn't been around anyone else enough for that attraction to develop.

Part of me wished I had her problem, because feeling something for two guys seemed almost worse.

A horn beeped as Lucas pulled up in his jeep with Kayla riding shotgun. Brittany was sitting in the back.

Connor opened the door for me, because, of course, he came from a family that did that sort of thing. I couldn't imagine Rafe extending the same courtesy. He'd probably think I could handle it myself. I climbed in. Connor tossed our backpacks into the rear of the jeep before sitting beside me.

"So what are we going to do about Bio-Chrome?" I asked.

"We stay alert," Lucas answered.

"You don't think we should be proactive, go after them?"

"Not until we know more."

I looked at Connor. He took my hand and kissed my knuckles. I felt Brittany shift on the seat beside me and my cheeks turned red.

"So I hear we're getting a new member for our team," I said casually.

"Yeah," Lucas said catching my gaze in the rearview window, before adjusting it slightly so he could see Brittany. "Daniel. He'll be joining us tomorrow."

"He's the guy from Seattle, right?" Kayla asked.

"That's right," Lucas said.

He'd become a Dark Guardian only this summer. We'd met him, of course, but we didn't know a lot about him.

I looked over at Brittany. She was staring out the window, as though she couldn't care less that an interesting new guy was part of our team.

"I'm glad we have another team member," I admitted. "With all those girls we're taking out tomorrow morning, the more help we have, the better."

Lucas cleared his throat. "Actually our number stayed the same. Rafe got reassigned."

I jerked my attention to Connor as his hand tightened around mine, before loosening again. "You didn't mention that."

"Is it important?" he asked quietly without looking at me.

That depended on the reason he'd been reassigned. It was, but only to me, and I couldn't admit that without explaining why. But as I watched Connor's jaw tighten, I had the sick feeling that he might already know the answer.

SIX

The national forest is a little over five million acres in size—about the size of New Jersey—and traveling from our hidden village to the main entrance of the park took us until late afternoon. It didn't help that we had to drive cautiously through the woods. Even when we eventually hit an actual road, we took it slow because of the wildlife that was likely to dart out in front of us—and maybe because in a way the wilderness we'd grown up in no longer felt like ours, no longer felt completely safe.

Ever since our encounter with Bio-Chrome we couldn't completely relax and enjoy our surroundings. We were waiting for them to leap out at us at every turn.

And I couldn't stop worrying about Rafe. I wanted to know what had really prompted his reassignment and if he was okay with it. I was so tense by the time Lucas brought the vehicle to a stop that I thought I might snap in two.

Inside the entrance to the park was a small village with a few cabins where the sherpas stayed when we weren't serving as guides. I shared one with Kayla and Brittany. After we dropped our packs in our cabin, we climbed back into Lucas's jeep to head to town. We were all restless, so we decided to spend some time at our favorite hangout—the Sly Fox.

The rustic building was a cliché: a bikers' bar and gaming hall, a favorite haunt of hikers, campers, and locals. The only people over age thirty were the owner, Mitch—who carded everyone multiple times—and a couple of the waitresses, who'd been around since the dawn of time and called everyone "Sugar."

I slid into a horseshoe-shaped booth in the back corner. Connor nudged up against me. As Kayla settled in on the other side of me, with Lucas beside her, Brittany said, "I'm gonna go shoot some pool."

"Aren't you hungry?" Connor asked.

"Not really. I'll catch you later."

She caught a guy's attention at the bar, and he followed her into the pool room. He was tall, with lanky black hair and a couple of days' beard growth.

"Who's that?" I asked.

"I don't know," Connor said. "I've never seen him before."

"Considering everything that's going on, shouldn't we be wary of strangers?"

"I don't think we want to get paranoid," Lucas said.

"It's not being paranoid when you're actually in danger," I pointed out. "There are a lot of people in here I don't recognize."

"It's summer. Tourist season."

Connor ran his hand along my shoulder. "Lucas is right. We can't suspect everyone."

But suspecting no one seemed equally dangerous to me.

After we gave our order to the waitress—burgers rare and fries all the way around—I relaxed against Connor. We'd spent several months apart while he'd been away at college. Maybe that was partly responsible for the strangeness I was feeling with him. Maybe we just needed to get back in sync. He put his arm around me and started toying with my hair. He always liked messing with my hair. He nuzzled my neck.

"Connor," I whispered.

"What?"

"We're in public."

"So? It's dark over here." He tipped his head to the side. Kayla and Lucas were talking low and snuggling, acting as though they were totally alone. "I've missed you, Lindsey. It just seems like we haven't really had any time together. We're taking another group out tomorrow. Have to be all responsible." He wrapped his hand around my neck and stroked the underside of my chin with his thumb, causing shivers of delight to race through me.

"It's really hard with you being away at college," I admitted.

"One more year, and you'll be there. Right?"

"I hope so. I'm losing my enthusiasm for school. I seem to be losing my enthusiasm for everything lately."

"Including me?"

I released a self-conscious laugh. "No." Then I thought about how strained things seemed to be between us lately and a thought occurred to me. "Are you interested in someone else? I mean, did you meet someone while you were away at school?"

"No. But things *are* different between us. I'm not sure what it is." He lifted my hair and nuzzled my neck again. "And it bothers me that I can't read your thoughts."

I felt the heat of his lips against my neck and went with it, drifting into a languid place where everything felt good. "You mean when you're in wolf form?"

"No. Like now, when I'm in human form. Lucas can

read Kayla's mind anytime, regardless of his form."

"What?" I jerked back. "Is that true, Lucas?"

He moved away from Kayla's lips as though I'd just woken him up. "Is what true?"

"You can read Kayla's mind even when you're not . . ." I glanced around. A guy at the bar jerked his gaze from us to his mug. Had he been watching us? Who was he? He gave me the creeps. He was big, with a shaved head and barbed wire tattoos around his biceps. He looked like someone who might have just stepped out of prison. Definitely not a lab tech . . . but who knows? I shifted my attention back to Lucas. "You know."

I didn't want to say *a wolf* aloud. Not everyone here was one of us, so we always had to be careful about what we said when we were here.

Lucas shrugged and leaned forward, across the table. Quietly, he said, "We can both read each other's thoughts anytime."

"Eww! You'd never be able to have a private thought."

"We can sense when the other wants privacy. We turn it off," Kayla said.

I looked at Connor worriedly. "Is that the way it's supposed to be? My parents never told me that."

"Mine didn't mention it either. Maybe it's like sex. They're not comfortable talking about it."

"Actually," Lucas began, "I think every bond is

different. The first time I saw Kayla it was like I was standing too close to a bug zapper."

"Oh, that's romantic," I said, while Connor chuckled gleefully at the gross image.

"It was like an electric charge," Lucas explained. "It wasn't unpleasant, but it was . . . a little unsettling."

"No matter the species, it seems guys are all alike," Kayla said, smiling. "Shy about the *L*-word."

"I'm not," Connor said. "I've loved Lindsey ever since she bloodied my nose because I took her chew toy."

My heart stuttered at his casual use of the *L*-word. In our relationship I was the one who was shy about using it. I always had been. I adored Connor, but I wasn't sure I'd ever told him I loved him. Now certainly wasn't the time. I slapped his arm playfully. "It was a teething ring and I was only a year old. I don't even remember it. But my parents always bring it up anytime our families get together."

"That and the naked videos."

"What's this?" Kayla asked, laughing.

I groaned. "I was two, Connor was four. We'd been playing in a splash pool. We took off our clothes and got in the sandbox. Makes sense to me. You don't get in a sandbox with wet clothes on."

"And I haven't seen her naked since," Connor said.

But he would. During my first transformation. Clothes hamper our ability to transform. Despite what happens to the Incredible Hulk, shirts don't rip off and pants don't stretch. I felt myself blush as Connor wiggled his blond eyebrows at me. For a species that had to divest itself of its clothing under what we considered *natural* circumstances, we were a modest bunch.

Thank goodness, the waitress brought our burgers over and conversation stopped as we wolfed them down. So to speak. Generally, we enjoyed nothing as much as we did warm, red meat. Although I did also have a weakness for fudge and anything else remotely chocolate.

When we finished eating, Connor and I decided to join Brittany in the pool room to give Lucas and Kayla some privacy. Walking inside, I was disappointed to see that all the tables were occupied. At the one nearest to the door, the young guy leaning over the table about to make his shot looked up and met Connor's gaze. With a shrug, he laid his cue stick down, bumped his partner on the shoulder—who set his stick on the table—and they both leaned against the wall, arms crossed defensively over their chests. Their reactions told me two things: they weren't yet eighteen and they were one of us, because apparently they recognized an alpha wolf when they spotted one. It was like that with our kind. Until we had the ability to go all furry, we gave way to those who could. It was a sign of respect.

A Static might have felt sorry for the two guys. After all, they were there first. But in order for our culture to work, a hierarchy had been established. As a Dark Guardian, Connor was at the top of the food chain. I had to admit that I felt a swelling of pride as he put his hand on the small of my back and led me to the table.

"I'll rack, you break," he said as he began taking the balls out of the pockets and rolling them toward one end.

I picked up the cue stick the first guy had set down. It was the right size for me. As I began chalking it up, I shifted my gaze over to Brittany. She'd finished whipping the butt of the guy who'd followed her into the room—or maybe he'd let her win so she'd relax around him. They began to set up for another game.

"What's wrong?" Connor asked quietly as he slid his arm around me and pulled me close. A possessive move. His question seemed to be a frequent one lately.

"I don't know. That guy. I'm not getting good vibes off him. He's not one of us."

"A hiker maybe. Mountain climber."

"A spy," I added.

"I think he's harmless."

"That's what we thought about Mason." He'd managed to capture Lucas in wolf form. If not for Kayla, Lucas might still be living in a cage somewhere, on display like a prized possession.

"Good point." He looked over at the young guys. It seemed to me that they had stopped breathing, waiting for his assessment. "Thanks for the table, but we changed our mind. We're going to play with a friend."

Brittany was leaning provocatively over the table when we arrived. She swept her gaze slowly over Connor, before taking her shot—and missing the corner pocket she'd been aiming for.

"All right!" the stranger said, with a grin. "Maybe this time I have a chance of winning."

He handed his beer bottle to her, before taking up his position to make a shot. With a dare in her eyes directed at me, she took a swig.

"You'll get kicked out if Mitch finds out you're drinking," I told her.

"He has to catch me first, and he's busy." She took another swallow, before tipping the bottle toward the guy lining up his shot. "This is Dallas. He's new to the area, here to do some hiking. These are my friends, Lindsey and Connor. They're destined for each other." Her words were almost slurred, and I wondered how much beer she'd had.

"Cool," Dallas said, amused. He nodded at me and touched two fingers to his brow in a salute to Connor, then sent two balls flying into opposite side pockets.

"He's also very good at pool. Game over," Brittany said.

"You don't know that," Dallas responded as he

pocketed another ball. "I could miss if you come over and distract me."

Smiling, Brittany shook her head. Maybe the reason none of the guys declared for her was because she gave the impression she was unavailable. She never flirted with anyone.

"Thought we could team up, challenge you guys," Connor said.

"Sure. Nothing like a friendly game to get to know each other better. Let me just finish up here." And Dallas quickly cleared the table of balls.

"See?" Brittany asked. "You guys don't stand a chance."

"We'll see," Connor muttered beneath his breath.

Our kind was nothing if not competitive.

While Connor and Dallas each rolled a ball across the table—whoever got it to stop closest to the far end would break—I nudged up against Brittany and said in a low voice, "So what's his story?"

"Says he's a hiker."

"You believe him?"

"No way, too pale."

"One of Mason's minions?"

"Maybe."

Nothing like spending all day in a lab to prevent a tan.

Connor won the right to break, and I felt that little

spark of pride again. My guy. But as he made his move to strike the balls, I shifted my gaze over to Dallas. He was watching the room as though he was expecting trouble. I felt the wariness creep through me.

We were at a disadvantage. Our best warriors were here, but they wouldn't be able to shift in front of all these tourists. We'd worked diligently to keep our special abilities a secret. But now I felt as though we were walking around with big signs taped to our backs saying, *Caution: We shift at will.*

Even though I couldn't shift yet. Soon, though. Very soon.

Connor called my name, and I realized it was my turn to shoot. I moved over to stand beside him. He pointed toward a solid ball. "That should be an easy shot."

I nodded jerkily.

He put his hand on the small of my back. "Relax."

"I know it's totally irrational, because I have no evidence for it, but I can't shake the feeling that there's trouble coming," I whispered.

"We'll handle it."

I had this déjà vu moment from last summer when I'd been assigned my first group of campers to lead out into the wilderness. I'd been so worried that I'd do something to get one of them hurt. Connor was going with me. "If something happens, we'll handle it," he'd said. So calm. He never doubted his ability to take care of any situation.

With a nod, I bent over to line up my shot.

I knew the second Rafe walked into the room. I didn't know how I knew. I wasn't facing the door. It was just an awareness that shimmered through me. I glanced back over my shoulder to see him sauntering toward us.

"So who's winning?" he asked.

"No one yet," Brittany said, right before she made introductions.

I was acutely aware of Rafe studying Dallas—he didn't trust him either. So that made all of us.

"Play already, will you?" Brittany prodded. I bent back over and aligned my cue stick.

"You're not lined up right to make that shot," Rafe said quietly, and before I could react, he was behind me, his arms coming around me. Everything within me went still. I wondered if he'd felt this same awakening when I'd been holding him on the bike last night.

I heard a low rumble. Anyone else might have mistaken the sound for someone clearing his throat, but I recognized it immediately as a warning growl coming from Connor. Completely ignoring him, Rafe adjusted my position slightly.

"You want to tap it low," he said.

I nodded, feeling an acute sense of loss when he moved away. I smacked the white ball and watched as it knocked the solid-colored ball into a corner pocket.

"That might be cheating," Dallas said.

"I'll buy you a plate of buffalo wings to make up for it," Rafe said.

"Sounds fair."

Connor and I won the game fairly easily, which made me think that Dallas didn't even try. Perhaps he really was using the occasion to just observe us. When we were finished playing, we returned to the booth, where Lucas and Kayla were waiting for us. Introductions were made. As we took our seats in the horseshoe shape, Dallas ended up being hemmed in on both sides.

He didn't seem to realize the danger he was in, because he glanced around, smiled, and asked, "So are you the werewolves I've been hearing about?"

SEVEN

Everyone at our table went eerily still, the way a predator does in the wild right before leaping for its victim. Even my heart felt as though it had stopped.

Dallas released an uncomfortable laugh. "Just kidding. I've been hearing these crazy rumors about things that go on in this area. Then tonight, here are all these new faces. Thought maybe you had to hide away during certain phases of the moon or something."

"We were at a family reunion," Lucas said with a deadly calm that sent a shiver racing up my spine. I never wanted to be on his bad side. "Where'd you hear these rumors?"

"Around. Here and there. It's insane, right? I mean

the idea that someone could actually shift into another form." Dallas held out his hands and studied them as though he'd never seen them before. "I mean, how could that even happen? How could a body change so drastically?"

Very slowly he looked around the table as though we had the answer. We did, but we sure weren't going to share it.

"There are all kinds of crazy stories about things happening in the wilderness," Brittany explained gently, and I wondered if she liked him. I'd never seen her show that much interest in a guy. How weird it would be to love a Static. Could it even happen?

My thoughts were drifting away from the problem at hand. *Who was this guy, and what did he really want?*

"Werewolves, vampires, ghosts," Brittany continued. "People are always telling scary stories around campfires. But that's all they are. Stories."

Dallas laughed again, only this time it was laced with relief. "Yeah, I know that. Should have seen your faces, though. You looked at me like I was serious. It would be cool, though, don't you think? If the ability to change our shape really existed?"

"I'd want to be a horse," I said, hoping to take the subject even further away from the truth.

"Horses have to work too hard," Connor said, taking my hand and squeezing it. "A dog. Sleep all day."

"A cat," Brittany said. "Only I'm allergic to them. Would I be allergic to myself?"

Dallas gave a more relaxed laugh. "Okay, I get it already. I shouldn't listen to campfire tales." He winked at Brittany. "So how about another game of pool?"

Once he and Brittany were back in the pool room, those of us left at the table looked uncomfortably at each other.

"What was *that* all about?" Kayla finally asked.

Lucas slowly shook his head. "I'm not sure. Rafe, keep an eye on him, especially while he's with Brittany."

My gaze jumped over to Rafe so I could judge his reaction. As usual, he didn't give anything away. Neither did he look at me. He just gave Lucas a nod and slid out of the booth.

"Do you think he's dangerous?" I asked.

Lucas shook his head. "If he is, we can handle him."

When we left an hour later, the consensus was that Dallas was just a tourist drawn in by the myths of the forest. We'd seen it before—which was the reason that the people from Bio-Chrome had sneaked by us. We'd thought they were harmless, too.

Rafe was going to keep an eye on Dallas, but the rest of us headed for bed. We were scheduled for an early start the following day.

* * *

The next morning we gathered near our cabins to greet our scout group. More than a dozen girls were practically bouncing around with excitement at the thought of camping in the wilderness. Or maybe their enthusiasm was due to the fact that three of their guides were hot—and I wasn't referring to Kayla, Brittany, and me.

Lucas, Connor, and Daniel were checking each girl's backpack to make sure it was adjusted comfortably on her shoulders and wasn't too heavy. We sherpas would be carrying the heavy or cumbersome supplies.

"Daniel is cute," Kayla said.

He hadn't gone to school with us, since his family lived near Seattle, but he'd joined the Dark Guardians earlier in the summer, so we already knew him. I hadn't really paid much attention to him, though. He wore his black hair in a buzzed style, which was unusual. Most of the guys we knew wore their hair longer.

"Yeah, whatever," Brittany said.

"You know it could be your attitude keeping the guys away," I pointed out.

"I don't want a guy who doesn't *want* me."

"Maybe he *will* . . . if you give him a chance," Kayla said.

"Besides, the elders said you just have to have a guy with you. He doesn't have to be *the one*," I told her. "When the right one comes along, you can re-bond with him."

She gave me an impatient glare. "They don't *know* it'll work that way. I'm the first girl who might have to go through it alone. They're just guessing."

Well, obviously she wasn't the first. If we knew a girl could die if she went through her first transformation alone, then somewhere along the way a girl had gone through it alone. But I thought it best not to point out that part. No reason to add to Brittany's worry.

"Of course they know what'll happen," I said, sounding more confident than I actually felt. Brittany might be giving me a hard time about my choices, but when all was said and done, we were friends. I wanted her to survive long past the next full moon. "They have the ancient texts, the books. They're bound to have used them to find an answer for this dilemma."

"You think?" she asked, and I heard the hope in her voice.

"Absolutely." I put my hand on her shoulder. "You're a Dark Guardian. They value you. They're not going to guess about something this important."

She shifted her gaze over to Daniel. He was crouched in front of three young scouts, explaining something to them. He had a broad, warm smile. Brittany sighed. "I guess I could do worse than him."

"That's the spirit!" I exclaimed. *Not*. Would I be as

difficult to please, as unwilling to settle, if I didn't already have Connor?

Brittany rolled her eyes. "You don't know what it's like. Lately I've been worried about. . . ." Her voice trailed off.

"Worried about what?"

"Nothing. Forget it."

Before I could convince her to tell me, she walked off into the group of girls and introduced herself to their leaders and chaperones.

I looked over at Kayla. Her face was set in a mask of worry.

"I have to believe she'll be okay," I told her.

Kayla gave me a soft smile. "I know. I had only forty-eight hours to prepare for my first full moon . . . I can't imagine how nerve-racking it must be for you to have a much longer countdown. But especially for Brittany."

A month ago I would have told her I couldn't wait. Now, I wasn't so sure.

"You said what you felt for Lucas was instantaneous—that you felt a strong bond immediately. Brittany has time to find someone."

Kayla nodded, but I suspected she didn't believe what I'd said about Brittany any more than I did. I didn't know what would be worse: to go through it alone or to go through it with someone who didn't really want to be there.

I looked back toward our group of girls. Brittany was actually talking to Daniel. Maybe there was hope for her after all.

Lucas gave the order for us to move out. I shifted my backpack and headed forward, bringing up the rear so I could make sure no little scouts got left behind or wandered off.

It seemed so odd not to have Rafe with us. I wondered where he was, what he was doing. I took a final, quick glance around, but I didn't see him anywhere. I trudged into the forest, surprised by how lonely I felt.

And wishing, with a ferocity that stunned me, that Rafe was with us.

By the time the sun was beginning to set, most of the girls had lost their exuberance. Not that I blamed them. Lucas had pushed us pretty hard.

Because we were supposed to be watching the girls and keeping an eye out for danger, we didn't pair up into couples until the camp was set up and everyone was seated around the campfire making our evening s'mores.

Kayla and Lucas were sitting close together, talking softly. It was obvious they were trying to behave in front of the young scouts, because they kept their touches brief and even those seemed inadvertent. But even when they weren't kissing or caressing, there was still an intimacy

90

between them—as though they shared the very deepest aspects of their souls.

Brittany, on the other hand, wasn't sharing even the outer edge of hers with Daniel. She sat beside him stiffly, concentrating on making her s'mores rather than talking with him. It was apparent that he felt awkward. Seeing them together, I couldn't imagine that a blind date would be any worse. At that moment I truly appreciated that I'd always had Connor.

Not that we were doing any talking or touching each other—inadvertently or otherwise. But at least we were acting comfortable around each other again.

The girls weren't talking much either. A couple of them looked as though they were going to drift off to sleep right where they were sitting.

I glanced surreptitiously at Brittany. "I don't think the elders should get into matchmaking," I murmured so only Connor could hear me.

"I've been thinking the same thing," he said, equally quiet. "It's a disaster."

I jerked my head around to stare at him. Out of the corner of my eye, I caught sight of Brittany suddenly studying me. I leaned in to Connor as though we were going to get cozy and whispered in his ear, "I don't think it's that bad."

He tucked some strands that had worked their way

out of my braid back behind my ear, his knuckles skimming my cheek, his eyes growing warm as though we were talking about personal things. "He's not even trying. I don't know. He could at least . . . talk to her."

I found it interesting that he thought Daniel was the problem while I thought it was Brittany's attitude.

"Maybe they just need a little more time to connect." I really wanted to stay positive regarding her chances of finding a mate.

"Man, I'm so glad I didn't have to do the whole dating scene."

I felt an uncomfortable tightening in my chest. "You don't think that's the reason we're together—because we were convenient—do you?"

"No." Leaning in, he kissed me tenderly.

One of the girls shrieked, then started to sing, "Connor and Lindsey, sitting in a tree . . ."

Connor and I broke apart so fast that I almost got whiplash.

Several other girls joined in. "K-i-s-s-i-n-g . . ."

Of course they ended the song wrong—they forgot to mention that after love comes transformation—but I decided not to correct them.

After that, it took their leaders a while to get them settled and into their tents. They decided to sing about Lucas and Kayla, then Brittany and Daniel. I'd never seen Brittany blush so much. I figured she would have run into the woods if she could have done it without looking cowardly.

Kayla was taking the first shift of the night watch, which left Brittany and me alone in our tent. We got ready for bed in silence. When the lights were out, I lay in my sleeping bag staring upward, thinking about Connor and wondering why we didn't cuddle more, why—far too often—simply talking seemed enough for us. Had we been together for so long that we'd grown immune to each other's bodies? Was I taking him for granted? Would I feel differently after I shifted?

I was already starting to notice some differences.

"Brit? Does the forest smell . . . richer to you?" I'd noticed fragrances during the day's hike in a way I never had before.

"What do you mean?" she asked.

"I can't explain it. Everything smells more alive. I know the change will bring on heightened senses—do you think it starts before the change?"

"Yeah, maybe . . . I mean, now that you mention it, yeah, things smell . . . bolder."

She said the words, but I didn't hear any commitment in them. Quite honestly, I didn't hear any truth. I rolled over to my side. "What do you think of Daniel? I mean, he seems nice."

"He's okay."

"You could try a little harder, you know."

"Easy for you to say. You've never had to *try*. You've always had Connor."

I thought about confessing that she might be right regarding what I had with Connor—and how convenience didn't necessarily mean we were right for each other. But as long as I didn't give voice to my doubts, they didn't seem real.

"I don't want to talk about Connor and me," I said, far more sharply than I'd intended.

"I don't want to talk about Daniel."

"Good night, then." I rolled over to my other side. Why was I even attempting to be nice, to help her with the selection of her mate? It wasn't really my business.

"Lindsey?" she called out hesitantly a few minutes later.

I almost didn't answer, almost pretended that I'd already fallen asleep. "What?"

"What if . . . what if I'm not a Shifter?" she said in a small voice.

I bolted upright, too stunned by the concept to respond. Hadn't Connor wondered the same thing about her?

"What if that's the reason none of the guys can connect with me?" she continued. "What if there's something *wrong* with me?"

"Oh, Brittany, that's . . . that's just . . ." I didn't know what to say. "Of course you're a Shifter."

"I feel like all the guys just look through me. Even Daniel smiles at me the same way that he smiles at the Girl Scouts—like I'm cute, but nothing special. There's never any fire."

Fire? Was she referring to the scary thing I felt whenever Rafe was near? For the long term, wasn't it better to feel comfortable with someone, to feel in sync? Fire could burn you to a cinder. It was just lust, not love—wasn't it?

But my insecurities weren't what she needed. She needed reassurance.

"Look, Brittany, I'm sure it has nothing to do with you," I said, even though I wasn't sure at all. Even Connor had doubts, but this close to the first full moon after her seventeenth birthday wasn't the time to reinforce these crazy ideas. "We only have a small pool of guys working as sherpas. It stands to reason that eventually there's going to be a disconnect. God, your true mate could be . . . I don't know. In California, maybe, or Florida. And this year, so few came for the celebration. Any other time, you might have connected with someone there. It sucks, totally. But maybe Daniel could be a surrogate until the real thing comes along."

"The first time we shift is supposed to have an element of romance about it. I don't think I can settle for a guy holding my hand when I want him holding my body. I'd rather just go through it alone."

"You could die."

"Or maybe I'd liberate us from this archaic tradition."

You only think it's archaic because you don't have a mate. Personally, I didn't want to go through it alone. I wanted the magic of the transformation and the wonder of bonding that followed.

"Anyway, I've got two weeks to decide what to do," she said. "I'll figure something out."

She was back to sounding like the same defiant Brittany I knew. Everything would be okay. As I drifted off to sleep, I felt certain of it.

The night was dark. The moon had yet to rise. A slight breeze was blowing my hair around. Connor came up behind me, wrapped his arms around me, and kissed the nape of my neck. A tingle traveled down my spine. I leaned into him.

"Soon," he whispered near my ear. "Very soon."

I turned within the circle of his arms and welcomed his kiss. It was heated with passion. He skimmed his fingers up my bare arms, and wherever he touched, I felt scalded.

I heard crackling and popping. I grew so hot, I thought I would melt. Drawing back, I found myself staring into Rafe's brown eyes, not Connor's blue ones. Somehow, without me noticing, he'd changed. I could see him clearly now, because the trees surrounding us were ablaze, and great orange and red flames were leaping into the sky.

Ignoring the danger we were in, Rafe pulled me back into his arms and lowered his mouth to mine until we became the fire and were consumed. . . .

I woke up breathing heavily and sweating. I scrambled out of my sleeping bag and stumbled from the tent, welcoming the feel of the cool night air against my face. I'd slept in my clothes, so all I was missing were my shoes, but I was accustomed to going barefoot so I wasn't bothered by the ground beneath my bare feet.

Connor was standing near the fire. He took a step toward me. "You okay?"

Nodding jerkily, I started to comb my fingers through my hair and remembered that it was braided. Only in my dream had it been free. "Yeah, I'm fine. Just a bad dream." Although not in the traditional sense of nightmares. I was more afraid of myself and the images I was conjuring than I was of any monsters.

Kayla had been sitting on a log. She got up and walked over. "You're so pale. Are you sure you're okay?"

"Absolutely. Why don't you go to sleep? I'll finish your shift."

"Lucas thought we'd pay more attention if—"

"I know. Weren't keeping watch with our mate. Connor and I will behave."

She glanced over at him. He nodded and jerked his head toward our tent. With a shrug, she smiled and patted my shoulder. "All right, then. Thanks."

She disappeared into the tent.

Connor took my hand. "Come sit by the fire. You'll feel better."

I doubted that. "There was a fire in my dream. Everything around me was burning. Just hold me for a minute."

I didn't wait for him to give me an answer. I walked toward his outstretched arms, never doubting that he'd welcome me there. He'd been my rock forever.

I tilted my head back and gazed deeply into his blue eyes. I don't know what he read on my face, but he dipped his head and kissed me.

The kiss resembled nothing in the dream. It was pleasant and sweet and warm. It was reliable. It was constant. It was real.

The kiss in the dream . . . it was just . . . well, it was just a dream.

Connor led me over to the log where Kayla had been sitting. Once I was settled on it, he crouched in front of me and tucked some stray strands behind my ear.

I swallowed hard. "The summer solstice, when you

couldn't find me . . . I was with Rafe."

A sadness touched his eyes right before he said quietly, "I know."

"You caught his scent on me."

He nodded.

"Why didn't you say something?"

"You're either mine or you're not. If you're mine, I'll fight to keep you. If you're not . . . maybe I don't want to know."

I skimmed my fingers along his cheek. Unlike Rafe, he seldom had stubble. "Nothing happened. We just went for a ride on his bike. I needed to get away from the doom and gloom for a while."

"That's what Rafe said."

"You confronted him?"

"Of course. Actually that's what my dad and I disagreed on. He thought I should have challenged him."

"That's insane! You can't kill him just because he took me for a ride."

"Relax, Lindsey. I don't have any plans to challenge him. I like to believe we've become a little more civilized over the years and can settle many of our differences in human form, not wolf."

"But is that the reason he's no longer part of our sherpa team?"

"No. The elders really are worried about Brittany. If

she and Daniel don't click, they'll probably put someone else with us."

I thought about telling him that she wasn't feeling the connection with Daniel, but we still had a few days for things to change.

Suddenly the hairs on the nape of my neck prickled—and not in the nice way that they had in my dream.

"Connor, do you get the sense that we're being watched?"

"Yes."

My breathing slowed as I tried to figure out from which direction someone might be watching us.

Connor suddenly spun around. Two girls were peering out of their tent. They both released high-pitched giggles and ducked back inside.

Connor chuckled. "I don't remember ever being that young and silly."

"I don't think it was them," I said as I stood up. I turned in a slow circle, but the earlier sensation that I'd had was gone.

"They were all I picked up on." Connor scented the air. "Nothing unusual."

I couldn't shake off the feeling that there had been someone else. "Lucas was probably right. We shouldn't keep watch with someone we'd rather snuggle with or talk to."

Connor grinned. "He is wise, our leader. You keep

watch here. I'll circle the camp."

I knew he wasn't going to find anything. Whoever it was had left. But it didn't stop me from wondering who it had been and, more important, what that person wanted.

EIGHT

We trekked for two more days, leading the girls farther into the forest. There were parts of the national
forest where few people traveled, where there was more
wildlife and more danger, but we avoided those places
and helped the girls and their troop leaders set up their
final camp in a relatively safe place. After we finished
ensuring that the camp was secure, we had plenty
of daylight left, so we began preparing for our depar-
ture from the group. Brittany and Daniel would stay
behind with them. Normally, we'd have just left one
sherpa, but the elders had given orders to encourage
Brittany to bond with Daniel.

I didn't see it happening, but a few more days together couldn't hurt.

"We'll be back in plenty of time to have you at Wolford before the full moon," Lucas said to Brittany.

"Whatever," she responded, as though she was bored with the whole thing.

It was the most important night of our lives, and she acted like she couldn't be bothered. Grabbing her arm, I dragged her away from the group.

"Hey!" she protested, jerking free of my grasp.

"Brittany, you've got to snap out of this. Daniel is trying—"

"There's no connection. Zero. Zilch. He and I both know it. I'd rather go through it alone."

"Just think of him as a lifeline. He could be there . . . just in case."

"It can't be as painful as the guys say. And if Lucas was just a distraction for Kayla—thank you very much but I can find my own distraction. I'll be fine."

I gave her a big hug. "We'll both be fine," I whispered and hoped it was true.

We were able to make better time without all the supplies we'd been lugging and because we weren't herding more than a dozen rambunctious girls. We began to make our camp as sunset approached, and I realized that with any luck, we'd be back at the forest entrance by tomorrow night.

Lucas and Connor went off to capture a rabbit. Kayla was building a fire. I was restless.

"I'm going to go pick some blackberries," I said to Kayla as I grabbed a small container.

She twisted around to look at me. "Are you sure you should go off by yourself?"

"I saw brambles in some of the thickets we passed. They aren't far. I won't be long."

"Just be careful."

"Always."

I headed back in the direction from which we'd come. Funny thing was, the blackberries were farther away than I remembered, and they weren't quite on the trail. I slid into the gulley and clambered up the other side where I could see berries peeking out through the thicket. Carefully avoiding the thorns, I plucked one and popped it into my mouth. Wild berries were always tastier than anything found in a store.

The container was half full—I am an optimist—when I became acutely aware of a presence and the hairs on my arms lifted. As slowly as possible, I peered around and that's when I spotted it.

A mountain cougar.

"Nice kitty," I whispered beneath my breath, knowing I was in trouble. If my scent was that of a human, maybe he'd move on. But we Shifters smell like wild animals.

He gave a deep, throaty *purrrr* and bared incisors that could tear flesh from bone. Cautiously I shifted my weight, prepared to leap into the brambles and hoping the thorns would serve as a deterrent. My mouth was so dry that I couldn't have spit if my life depended on it. My heart was pounding so hard that I was surprised the others couldn't hear my blood *whoosh-whooshing* between my ears.

I saw the cat's muscles tense.

I leaped up and screamed just as he lunged.

A blur of movement knocked into the cat right before it slammed into me. I felt the heat of the bodies, the air rushing past with the force of the collision. I fell down and scrambled back, my gaze locked on the battle. I could see now that a wolf had attacked the cat. Not just any wolf. One I knew.

Rafe.

What was he doing here? And what if he lost this fight?

I got to my feet and took a step forward, a step back. I wanted to stop it. I didn't want Rafe getting hurt. My heart was racing. I wanted to scream for help, but I couldn't risk distracting him. My fists were closed so tightly that my nails were digging into my palms.

The cat's shrieks rent the air, quickly followed by the

wolf's growls. They were locked in combat. Swiping at each other, snarling, burying their teeth into each other. I could see that Rafe was bleeding. I wanted to rush over to him, to help him. I wanted him safe. I wanted the cat gone.

The cougar finally broke free and raced into the thickness of the forest. The wolf took a step toward me and collapsed.

I raced over, sat on the ground, and put his head on my lap. He was bleeding near his shoulder and his hindquarters. As he tried to lift his head, I pushed it back down, gently stroking his fur. "Shh, shh, just relax. You need to heal. You'll be all right."

Holding his gaze, I thought I'd never been so grateful for anyone's arrival, but it was more than the fact that he'd saved me from a cougar attack. I was just so glad to see him. I wanted to know what he'd been doing, how he was doing. I had a hundred questions for him, but mostly I just wanted to hold him. He licked my bare knee, as though he wanted to communicate that he was feeling the same. I didn't scold him for sneaking in a kiss.

I heard a twig snap and jerked my head up to see the guy who'd played pool with Brittany—Dallas—standing there.

"So what are you—the wolf whisperer?" he asked.

* * *

"I'm really trying not to freak out here," Dallas said. "But this is just . . . it's wild, man, it's totally unbelievable. Werewolves. They exist."

I hadn't seen any point in trying to lie my way out of a situation that couldn't get much worse. Rafe's clothes had been in a heap on the forest floor—explain that. His gaping, bleeding wounds had healed right before Dallas's eyes—again, explain that. I was holding a wolf in my lap and talking tenderly to him—yeah, normal people do that all the time.

So I'd led Dallas back to our camp. We'd been only a few minutes into the journey when Rafe had silently joined us in human form, fully clothed. Seeing him again like that was like a kick to the gut that almost made me giddy. I hadn't realized that I'd actually *missed* him, probably a lot more than I should have. I had the sense that he'd missed me too when he silently handed me my container of blackberries. It was full, which meant he'd taken the time to pick some before catching up with us.

Now we were sitting beside the fire, where two rabbits were cooking. I wasn't certain I'd be able to eat. Disaster seemed a heartbeat away.

"We prefer the term 'shapeshifters,'" Lucas said. "Werewolf is so . . . Hollywood."

"Didn't mean to offend, but God. Mason kept talking

about werewolves, and I just thought he was insane, that his brain power was too much for him. I mean, his IQ is off the charts."

"You know Mason Keane?" I blurted.

"Hard not to when I work—*worked*—for Bio-Chrome."

"'Worked'?" Lucas repeated, suspicion in his voice.

"Yeah. I quit about ten days ago. Decided to take a long-overdue vacation. And—okay, I was curious. I wanted to discover for myself if you really existed."

"And you decided to do that by following us?" Connor asked.

"Don't sound so offended, man. He was following me." He jerked his thumb toward Rafe. "Not that I ever spotted him or anything. It was just a sixth-sense kind of thing, you know?"

Yeah, I knew. So the odds were that when I had felt that sensation of being watched, it had been Dallas doing the watching. Or maybe it had been Rafe, slipping in to keep an eye on us.

"So why follow us?" Kayla asked.

"I'm a scientist. I need proof. So are all of you . . ." Dallas's voice trailed off as he glanced around.

"If we tell you that, then we'll have to kill you," Rafe said, and I thought he was only half joking.

"Look, dude, I'm not here with evil intentions. Like I said, I just wanted proof. And I was trying to figure out if I could trust you. For all I knew, you'd get rabid and slobber."

"And now you know we don't," Lucas said. "What's it to you?"

Kayla put her hand over his. I wondered if she was aware that Lucas was trying to decide what to do with the human. Worst case scenario involved death, but I didn't think we'd go there. We could take him to Wolford and let the elders deal with him. Or we could take our chances and just let him go. Who would believe him anyway?

"Look, I can feel the tension mounting so let's all relax, okay? I'm on your side. I figured if you really existed I should tell you what I know. And if you didn't exist, then I was working for some crazies and shouldn't even bother to ask them for a job reference."

"So what exactly do you know?" Connor asked.

"Right at the edge of the forest, just before you get to the part that's designated national park land, there's a wooded area that's still private property. Last year Bio-Chrome started building a lab there. Seemed an odd choice, you know? Because it's away from everything, in the middle of nowhere. Helicopters bring in our supplies. We live there; we work there. It's almost a prison. To be honest with you, I wasn't sure they were going to let me leave.

"Anyway, they're very secretive about what's going

on at the facility. When I applied for the job, all I knew was that it involved studying what they were calling the 'L-factor gene.' Stupid me, I thought maybe it referred to love . . . something to help geeky guys get dates. I really had no clue. It wasn't until I was working there that I discovered the *L* stood for *lycanthropy*. I thought it was a joke."

He stared into the fire. Whether he was trying to determine what more to tell us or still dealing with the fact that we actually existed, I didn't know.

"But Dr. Keane and Mason, they were so obsessed. They kept talking about how they wanted to capture a lycanthrope and study him. It sounded barbaric. I mean, if these beings did exist, locking them up would be taking away their rights. When I pointed that out, Mason said that lycanthropes weren't human, so they didn't have any rights. It just sounded so wrong."

But sounded so much like Mason, I thought. I glanced over at Kayla. She looked incredibly sad, and I knew it was because she didn't understand why everyone didn't accept our existence as gracefully as she had.

"Why didn't you tell us all this the other night?" Lucas asked.

Dallas met his gaze. "I was going to, but the more I talked, the more the idea of werewolves—sorry, I mean 'shapeshifters'—it just sounded so . . . out there." He studied his hands again, the way he had at the Sly Fox: as though he could figure out how we did it.

"So you thought spying on us was a better solution?" Connor asked.

"Look, I've never done this James Bond stuff before, okay? So shoot me. Besides, I saw what he's capable of." He pointed at Rafe. "You could kill me, but I stepped forward and here I am."

"Which brings us back to—exactly why are you here?" Lucas asked.

"I just thought you should know what they were planning."

"You said the lab was near the national forest. Where exactly?"

"Far northeast corner."

"Why don't you show us?" Lucas asked.

"What? Like on a map?"

Lucas was wearing his *don't-mess-with-me* expression. In it, I could see the ferocity that marked him as the leader of our pack. Judging by the way Dallas's eyes widened slightly, I suspected he recognized it, too.

"I was thinking you could show us in person," Lucas said.

"You don't trust me," Dallas said, his voice slightly petulant.

"Let's just say we've dealt with Bio-Chrome before.

The company is not exactly on our list as a friend of endangered species."

Suddenly appearing very nervous, Dallas glanced around. "They've hired mercenaries to guard the place. They look like they'd kill their grandmothers if the price was right."

"And you didn't think that was worth mentioning earlier?" Rafe asked with a deadly calm that sent a shiver up my back, even though I knew he'd never hurt me. He was studiously avoiding looking at me—while I was having a hell of a time keeping my gaze from wandering over to him.

"I was getting around to it. Look, I'm being a good samaritan here. And I'm feeling very unappreciated."

"You just have to show us the lab," Lucas reassured him. "We may have some questions once we see it."

Reluctantly, Dallas nodded. "Yeah, okay, I guess that makes sense. But listen, I took a room at the hotel in Tarrant. Left some of my stuff there. I want to pick it up before we head out, because once I show you the lab, I'm going to Canada."

Everyone else was looking at Dallas as though he was the enemy while I was viewing him as one of the good guys. I hope I wasn't being naive.

"You risked a lot to come and tell us about the lab," I said softly.

"Like I said, what they're doing . . . it's not right."

"We appreciate you coming forward," Lucas said, but his voice had an *I-still-don't-quite-trust-you* edge to it.

"Yeah," Dallas mumbled. "Just hope it doesn't get me killed."

I hoped it didn't get any of us killed.

Dallas had a little pup tent that he was going to set up, but Lucas convinced him to sleep in the guys' tent instead. Not that he could have slipped away without us noticing, because we were taking turns keeping watch.

I was lying on my back in my tent. Rafe was watching things now. Then it would be Kayla. I hadn't gotten a chance to talk with Rafe, to thank him for the blackberries—and for saving my life.

Very quietly and cautiously, I peeled back my sleeping bag, sat up, and tugged my shoes onto my feet.

"Where are you going?"

My heart leaped into my throat at Kayla's question.

"Can't sleep. I'm going to get some fresh air."

"Look, Lindsey, it's none of my business—"

"No, it's not," I interrupted, certain I knew where she was heading with this. And immediately I felt guilty with my impatience. "Look, I just . . . I need to be sure."

I didn't want to tell her about my dreams of Rafe or how thrilled I'd been to see him. Both of these things were wrong if I was committed to Connor. But I couldn't deny that I felt an excitement when Rafe was near. Was it just because he was novel and Connor was familiar?

"It's not fair to Connor," Kayla said.

"It'll be unfair if I take doubts into our future."

Without waiting for her to respond, I got up and walked out of our tent. I felt Rafe's presence before I even saw him. He was back in the shadows near our tent. I felt his gaze fall on me. There was so much power behind it, he might as well have touched me. I grew hot, just as I had in my dreams. I crossed my arms over my chest as I walked over to him, because I was afraid I wouldn't have the strength of will not to touch him.

"I wanted to thank you for the blackberries." It was an inadequate start to the conversation, but how could I explain that I'd just needed to see him again?

"The blackberries?" It sounded as though he'd shoved out the words through clenched teeth.

I swallowed hard. "And for saving my ass."

"I can't believe"—he shook his head before continuing—"I can't believe you went off by yourself."

"These are my woods," I stated emphatically. "*Our* woods. I've always felt safe in them."

"They're not safe anymore. Don't you get it?" he whispered harshly. "If anything had happened to you, if I hadn't been there—it would have killed me."

Before I realized what he intended to do, he grabbed me, pulled me to him, and slashed his mouth across mine, kissing me with a ferocity that left me shaking and clinging to him as though I were suddenly drowning and he were my only hope.

I'd always thought a kiss was just a kiss. I'd been wrong. My body responded with a wild thrumming—I was a string on a harp that had been plucked and was now vibrating with a sweet sound. The kiss was hotter than any I'd ever received from Connor.

Or maybe it was just that the chemistry between Rafe and me was different. I wound my arms around his neck and pressed up against him. He drew me even closer to him, with one arm against my back and his other hand threading its way through the tangle of my hair. It seemed like he intended never to let me go. We were so close together that I wasn't sure where my body ended and his started. Moonlight couldn't have seeped between us.

Even as I relished the incredible pleasure pouring through me, my mind was screaming that this was wrong, so wrong. I belonged to Connor. I was his. It was decided.

I broke off the kiss and staggered backward. Breathing heavily I stared at Rafe, trying to understand what had just happened. He held out a hand toward me. "Lindsey—"

"No," I whispered. Whatever he was going to say, I

didn't want to hear it. "That was wrong."

Turning on my heel, I raced back to my tent with the truth pounding through my mind. There were things in the forest more dangerous than cougars, more dangerous even than Bio-Chrome.

NINE

It was nearly dark the next night when we finally reached the entrance to the park. I'd spent the entire day avoiding looking at Rafe, like I was afraid that I'd burst into flames if we made eye contact or that Connor would somehow find out Rafe and I had kissed.

I felt as though I needed a more powerful word to describe what had happened last night—*kiss* just didn't cut it. The intensity of the encounter was probably just brought on by fear and relief and the whisper of danger that surrounded us. But still, it had left me shaken and unsettled.

"So it's agreed? You're going to go with Rafe tomorrow, show him the lab?" Lucas asked as we gathered at the park entrance.

"Yeah, dude, sure," Dallas replied.

"I have a motorbike," Rafe said. "We should be able to make good time. How about I meet you at dawn?"

"I'm not really an up-at-dawn kinda guy," Dallas said. "How about mid-morning?"

They agreed on a time, and Rafe left with Dallas. I wondered if he planned to keep watch over the ex-Bio-Chrome employee all night. Kayla and I had a group of bird watchers to take out the following morning. Lucas had decided that he and Connor should go to Wolford and talk with the elders.

"We'll leave in the morning," Connor told me. "Want to catch a movie tonight?"

I nodded, trying to sound enthusiastic when I said, "Yeah."

I needed some Connor time, desperately, but I was so afraid that he was going to discover my lapse in loyalty the night before. Even if adrenaline *had* brought on the kiss, I should have been strong enough to resist. My problem was that I wasn't sure I'd *wanted* to resist.

It was with a sense of relief that I walked into my cabin, as though four walls could somehow protect me from myself, from these never-before-felt feelings I had toward Rafe. It didn't help that Kayla had been studying me all day as though she expected me to break at any moment.

"Something happened last night when you went to

talk to Rafe, didn't it?" she asked as she dropped her backpack on her bed.

"Don't have time to talk about it. Connor and I have a date." I walked into the bathroom and took a hot shower. Starting tomorrow, I'd have a couple of days without Connor or Rafe. Alone with my thoughts, maybe I could figure things out.

Meanwhile, I wanted to look my best for Connor, but for some reason I wasn't satisfied with anything I did. My hair was flat, my makeup boring. The saving grace was my outfit: a short white skirt, a purple strapless top, and my white denim jacket. I even wore sandals with short heels. They made me feel sexy.

Judging by the low whistle that Connor gave when I stepped outside, he agreed. It made me feel a little less guilty about what had happened the night before.

The moon was a little larger and brighter tonight. Connor and I decided to walk to town. It would mean catching a later movie, but I was more interested in our being together than in what movie we were going to watch. Holding hands, we walked along in companionable silence. I tried not to think about Rafe but I was worried about him going off to find the Bio-Chrome lab by himself. Well, not *totally* by himself, of course. Dallas would be with him, but I didn't see him as being much of a fighter if they got into trouble.

"What if this thing with Dallas is a trap?" I asked. "If they need one of us . . . we're handing them Rafe on a silver platter."

Connor's fingers tightened around mine. "Major rule tonight: We can't talk about Bio-Chrome or any of this other stuff that's happening. Just for a few hours, let's pretend everything is normal."

It hadn't occurred to me that I wasn't the only one craving the safety of the world we'd lived in before. But he was right. We were trying to escape from reality for a few hours.

"Okay, then. What movie is showing, anyway?" I asked. Tarrant had a small theater that showed only one movie at a time.

His smile flashed white in the near darkness. "Something with Reese Witherspoon—which means a chick movie. You're going to owe me big-time for this."

"Going to a movie was *your* idea," I felt the need to point out, punching his arm playfully.

"Ow!" He rubbed his arm, then pulled me off the road into the shadows of the trees, until my back was pressed against bark. "You know, Lindsey, you've shared every moment of my life, big and small."

"Not your first transformation."

"You would have been there if it were allowed. I want to be there for you, for your first time. I love you."

My heart slammed against my ribs, but not for the

reasons it should have. I should have felt joy, but instead I was hit with terror at the enormity of what Connor had said and at my inability to return such a heartfelt sentiment. Either Connor was aware of my inner struggle or he wasn't expecting a reply from me because his mouth covered mine. His kiss had never seemed so important, so significant, because it had never followed those three little words that were so monstrously huge.

I fought not to compare it to the unexpected kiss I'd had last night—the one that had stolen my breath and left me trembling.

Connor pulled back. I could sense tenseness in him as his hands closed around my arms. "You're thinking about Rafe."

"What? No."

"Tell me you love me."

"You know I do."

He released a short burst of hard laughter and stepped away from me. "Do you love him?"

I felt tears burning my eyes. "Connor, let's not do this."

"Do. You. Love. *Him*."

I'd always been able to talk to Connor about anything. Suddenly it was so hard to force out the words. "I don't know."

"God, Lindsey, your transformation moon is coming

up and you don't know? Don't you think you need to know?"

"What do you suggest? I go to the movies with him?"

A heavy silence descended as though I'd dropped a bomb and we were waiting for it to explode.

"How do you know that I'm the right one, Connor?" I asked, hating that my voice sounded so small, so unsure.

"I just know."

"That's not an answer. *How do you know?*"

He took several steps away and then came back toward me. "Yeah, okay. Maybe you do need to go out with him."

My heart thumped; I was panicking with the possibility that we were breaking up. Was this what I wanted? I honestly didn't know any more. "Are you serious?"

"Yeah, I think I am."

He started to walk away.

"Connor, wait!" I hurried after him. "I don't want things to end—"

I came to an abrupt halt. The hairs on the nape of my neck began to prickle with the weird sensation you get when something just isn't right.

"Connor!" I whispered harshly, loud enough for him to not only hear me but to detect the dread in my voice as well. Before I knew it, he was back at my side, emitting a low, throaty growl.

"Do you feel it?" I asked. It felt like . . . a disharmony in the universe—which makes me sound like some sort of New Age guru or something, but I don't know how else to explain it. The forest just felt . . . *wrong*.

I heard Connor inhale deeply.

"Blood," he said in a low voice. "A lot of it. Still warm. Maybe a recent kill. Or someone badly wounded."

"*Someone?* Maybe it's an animal."

"Definitely human."

My stomach roiled at the thought of who might be out there, wounded and possibly dying. I knew we had to find out what had happened—and Connor knew it, too.

He took my hand, our fight apparently forgotten. "Are you sure you're going to be okay with this?"

"Of course." In fact, I actually *wasn't* sure, but no way was I going to admit it.

He released my hand, and I was aware of his movement and his clothes being shoved into my arms.

"What if it's a trap?" I asked.

"It's human blood, Lindsey. Someone might be hurt." And he could find whomever it was far more quickly in wolf form. "We won't be able to communicate, so just stay close. If you think there's a danger to you, run as fast as you can. Holler to get attention if you have to."

"Got it."

He quickly brushed his lips over mine, and I could

123

only hope that it wasn't the last kiss we'd ever share. *Could I be any more confused? One minute I'm not sure we should be together and the next I'm hoping that kiss wasn't the last.*

A sort of electricity filled the air, and then fur was brushing up against me. Connor wasn't too difficult to see in the dark because his fur was pale blond in color, a little darker than my hair. As a wolf he was able to read my thoughts, so I focused on the task before us. I brushed my hand along his fur. As he began to walk, sniffing the ground and air, I remained close enough so I wouldn't lose him, my fingers occasionally sifting through his fur.

So I was very much aware when he suddenly bristled, as though whatever we were searching for, he had found. I could smell it now, the metallic odor saturating the air so thickly that it made me queasy. I could see a shadowed form lying prone on the ground.

Connor released a long, low howl. I didn't know why the call of the wolf could carry so far and so effectively. I could be screaming bloody murder and few would hear me to come and help, but many of our kind would hear Connor. They would come. And with any luck, they'd bring flashlights. A lot of information could be communicated in a howl.

Connor was suddenly hairless, and my fingers were touching his warm, bare shoulder. He was in a crouched position. "He's dead," he said somberly.

"Who is it?" I dared to ask.

"Dallas. I recognized his scent a while back, and my night vision is good enough that I can see him clearly now."

Stunned, I was barely aware of a tug on the clothes I held in my arms. I released them. The inside of my mind was screaming, *Who would do this? Why would they do it?* Only one answer came to mind: Bio-Chrome.

Connor wrapped his arms around me. He'd put his jeans back on, but he was shirtless. I could feel the warmth of his skin against my cheek.

"You okay?" he asked.

With him so near, I could now ask for the answer I'd been dreading. "How did he die?"

Connor's hold on me tightened as though he needed as much comfort as I did. "Looks like someone—or something—ripped out his throat."

TEN

Connor hadn't put his shirt back on because he'd draped it over Dallas's face and shoulders. When Lucas, Rafe, and Zander, another Shifter, arrived with flashlights to illuminate the grim scene, I was grateful to see nothing more gruesome than a stained, hunter-green T-shirt.

"You didn't notice anyone around here?" Lucas asked.

"No," Connor responded.

I felt a touch on my arm and jerked my head to the side. It was Rafe. I couldn't believe how glad I was to see him, to know for sure that he was all right. His gaze wandered slowly over me as though he wanted to make sure that it wasn't any of my blood tainting the air.

"Are you okay?" he asked, his voice raspier than usual, the way mine got when I had a scare.

I nodded quickly—too quickly. "Yeah, I just . . . I'm okay."

He left my side then, and I felt keenly the loss of his presence. He knelt down and peered beneath the T-shirt. "Looks like the real deal," Rafe said.

He was referring to the bite—it was real, not a wound that someone had made so it would look as though Dallas had been attacked by a wolf.

"Thought you were supposed to be watching him," Connor said, irritation in his voice. I wasn't convinced it was just because Rafe had neglected his duties.

"We were going to grab a burger at the Sly Fox, but he wanted to shower first. I didn't think I needed to sit in his room, so I went to wait for him at the bar. When he didn't show, I went back to the hotel. He wasn't there."

"I wonder what happened," I murmured.

"Maybe someone figured out he wanted to help us—and didn't like it," Rafe said, his voice sympathetic. I felt the force of his gaze on me and knew I should probably look away, but I couldn't. "The clerk at the desk said some big dude had been looking for him."

"One of the mercenaries from Bio-Chrome?" I asked, my voice low.

"That'd be my guess. If so, looks like he found him."

"We need to alert the sheriff," Lucas said.

"Do we want to get the police involved?" Rafe asked.

"I don't see that we have a choice. He's not one of ours. He could have family somewhere."

Sheriff Riley, however, *was* one of ours. He'd play this any way he could in order to keep the press low-key and to ensure the *National Enquirer* didn't start poking around for a story on rabid wolves or werewolves that tore out the throats of unsuspecting tourists.

"I'm going to take Lindsey back to her cabin," Connor said.

"Okay," Lucas said, distracted, staring at the body.

I didn't remember anything about the walk back to my cabin, except that it had been silent. The owls weren't even hooting. It was as though the entire forest had gone into mourning.

When we got to my cabin, I opened the door and walked in. Connor followed.

Kayla was sitting up in bed. She threw back the covers and hurried over to me. I wondered what my face showed— maybe she saw that all the blood had drained from it. I felt like a walking zombie. "Are you okay?" she asked.

I was beginning to think that was the dumbest question in the entire world. Why would people ask that when it was obvious I wasn't?

"Tell her, okay?" I asked Connor. "I want to take a shower."

I strolled into the bathroom and closed the door. I

turned the knob on the shower as far as it would go in the direction of hot water. It was summer and the nights were cool, but I felt as though I'd just walked across the frozen tundra. Without removing my clothes, I stepped into the shower, sat on the floor, and just let the water slam into me. I felt like the scent of blood had saturated my skin and clothing. I drew up my legs, wrapped my arms around them, pressed my forehead to my knees, and started to cry.

As a rule, I wasn't much of a crier. But Dallas hadn't seemed like a bad guy. He wanted to help us. Why hadn't we realized the risk he was taking? We'd met several of the Bio-Chrome scientists—they cared about one thing and one thing only: getting to the root of our DNA.

I heard the door open and a bit of coolness seeped into the room that was now cloudy with steam. I was probably scalding myself, but I seemed incapable of feeling anything.

"Lindsey?" Kayla asked as she drew the curtain aside just a bit.

"Please don't ask me if I'm okay," I insisted.

"I won't." She reached over and turned off the water. "Let's get you dry."

"I can do it." Somehow I did. I managed to get out of my wet clothes, dry off, and put on the pajamas she'd set on the counter for me. When I was finished, I left the bathroom and crawled into my bed beside hers.

"Where's Connor?" I asked.

"He left. He wanted to go back and help Lucas figure out what happened." She sat on the edge of my bed. "Do you want to talk about it?"

"Not really."

"When my parents were killed, I didn't talk about it," Kayla said. "That kind of trauma can mess with your head."

"We barely knew the guy," I reminded her. "But he seemed nice." It didn't even sound like me talking. Where were these words coming from?

"Connor said he doesn't think it was a random animal attack. He thinks it was murder," Kayla said. "Either one of us has gone over to the dark side, or one of the Bio-Chrome people has a trained dog or wolf."

"We were the only ones who knew he was going to help us," I said. But I couldn't help but believe that Bio-Chrome was involved.

I was still cold. I slipped further beneath the blankets and looked at Kayla. "I guess we'll find the answers when we find that Bio-Chrome lab," I said.

"I wonder how much harder that's going to be now."

"I don't know, but hard isn't impossible. At least we know the direction to go in."

"Unless he lied," Kayla said quietly. "Maybe his mission was to put us off track."

"Well, we can't solve the mystery tonight. I'm going to sleep."

"Are you sure you're—"

"I'm totally fine," I answered before she could finish. I rolled over, giving her my back. I heard her bed creak as she settled in. Then the lamp between our beds was clicked off.

I lay there for the longest time, exhausted but unable to sleep. I was acutely aware of Kayla becoming absolutely still. She was never restless in sleep. Then I sensed something beyond the door—a scuffling sound, like someone had stepped onto the porch.

Slipping out of bed, I crept barefoot across the cabin and slowly, quietly opened the door. I stepped onto the porch and drew the door closed. I wasn't sure how I knew it would be Rafe there. I just knew. I wanted to walk into his embrace, to hold him and let him hold me. I thought about the argument Connor and I had been having. Did he mean what he'd said? Was he right? Did I need to explore these feelings I had for Rafe?

"I didn't mean to wake you," Rafe said quietly, standing with his hands shoved into the pockets of his jeans.

"You didn't."

"I wanted to make sure you were all right."

I felt the tears sting my eyes. "Rafe, I think maybe it's my fault he was killed."

"What? No." Reaching out, he tenderly skimmed his fingers along my cheek. "If it's anyone's fault, it's mine."

"But if I hadn't gone to look for blackberries, if he hadn't seen you in wolf form—"

He touched his finger to my lips to silence me, then drew me up against him. I drew comfort from his hands stroking my back.

"If he'd told us everything that first night, things might have gone differently. We'll never know. Things played out the way they did, but none of us had control over that. The only thing we know for sure is that someone was looking for him and now he's dead. But you can't carry that burden."

I could if I wanted, but I didn't say anything because I didn't want to argue with him. I'd had enough tension for one night. Right now, being in his arms was as relaxing as getting a massage at my mother's spa.

"Listen, last night—when I kissed you," he said softly, "I'm sorry if I upset you. I was just so scared when I saw that cougar . . . I just needed more than to hold you, to know you were okay. If I'd been able to talk to you right after, it might have been different, but what I was feeling . . . it had been building—"

"It's okay." I cut him off before he said something that either of us would regret.

He pressed a kiss to my forehead, then reluctantly, he

released his hold on me and stepped back. "Well, like I said, I just wanted to make sure you were okay before I headed out."

"Where are you going?"

"To find that lab."

My heart hammered against my chest. "Are Connor and Lucas going with you?"

"No, they've gone to meet with the elders. They'll be back sometime tomorrow. I'm leaving now."

"I want to go with you."

"No, it's too dangerous."

"Rafe, I feel like it's my fault Dallas is dead. I'll go search for the lab by myself if I have to."

He released a frustrated sigh. "Lindsey, this isn't going to be like leaving camp to look for blackberries."

"I know that. I want to do this."

"Connor won't like it."

Connor was the one who'd told me that maybe I needed to go out with Rafe. I knew that this wasn't what he had in mind, but still, he couldn't get too angry at me. This way, I could help *as well as* spend a little time with Rafe, as he'd suggested. "I have to do this."

Rafe paused for what seemed like a long time.

"Okay. You've got ten minutes to pack."

Nodding, I reached back for the door.

"Lindsey?"

I glanced back over my shoulder at him.

"Do you ever wonder if it's worth it—the price we pay to keep our existence a secret?"

"I wonder a lot of things, Rafe." *Mostly about you and me and what this strong feeling truly is that I hold for you. Is it infatuation with the forbidden? Or is it something more?*

ELEVEN

It's not easy to sneak out of your cabin when one of your roommates has recently had her first transformation and her senses are heightened.

"What are you doing?" Kayla asked sleepily as she sat up.

I hadn't turned on a light, but an outside light that lit the area seeped into our room through the curtained window as I packed my things. "Nothing. Go back to sleep."

"Obviously *something* is up."

During the past year, Kayla had become my best friend while my relationship with Brittany had started to become as strained as the one I had with Connor. I knew someone needed to know where I was going, and I believed I could trust her. "I'm going with Rafe to look for the hidden lab."

The bedroom lamp suddenly came on, and Kayla was staring at me through narrowed eyes. "We're supposed to take out another group tomorrow."

"They're bird watchers. They're only here for the day. You'll be fine without me."

She combed her fingers through her thick, curly red hair and shook it out. "Rafe could probably search faster without you, don't you think?"

She was right; he could. Would I be hindering him? Was it really my desire to help that had me volunteering to go with him? Or was it something more selfish than that?

"I'm feeling guilty about Dallas. I didn't really trust him, but he may have died because he was bringing us information."

"This is me, Lindsey. The truth?"

"That *is* the truth. Just not all of it." I sighed and looked at my watch. I only had a few minutes, but I really needed to share all these doubts I had about my destined mate. Sitting on the edge of my bed, I tried to calm my pounding heart. I'd never said this out loud to anyone—not even to myself. Facing my true feelings was terrifying. "Kayla, lately I can't stop thinking about Rafe. I have these intense dreams about him. And last night he kissed me."

"In your dream?"

I shook my head. "No—for real. And it was . . . amazing. Powerful. Feral. I don't want to hurt Connor, but I need to figure out what it is I'm feeling for Rafe. It's not like anything I've ever experienced before. It fills me with wonder but at the same time it terrifies me."

"Do you love Connor?"

I dropped my head back and stared at the planks in the ceiling, imagining I could see Connor's face in a knot in the wood. "I do, but . . ."

"But . . . ?"

I lowered my gaze to meet hers. "What's it like to love Lucas?"

Her brow pleated. "Intense. Consuming. I have no doubt that he's my mate."

"That's my problem. I care for Connor, but I *do* have doubts. And he knows it. We were fighting about it right before we found Dallas. He wants me to confront whatever it is I'm feeling for Rafe, but I can't do that without spending time with Rafe. And the full moon . . . it's not going to wait for me to decide. It's going to come—*soon*—and I have to know. Maybe a few days in the woods with Rafe will help me figure out what I feel for both of them.

And we'll be doing something good at the same time."

"Lindsey, this is reckless. It's way too dangerous."

It was—in so many ways.

"I know, but I have to take the risk." Not only to find the lab, but also to discover what was truly in my heart.

"What if you decide . . . and it's not Connor?"

I felt a painful tightness in my chest. I didn't want to hurt him. "Would it be fair to him if I accept him as my mate, but I didn't love him like you love Lucas?"

Kayla got up, crossed over to me, and hugged me tightly. "It wouldn't be fair to either of you. If you can't decide, *I'll* be there with you for the change."

"But you're bound to Lucas."

"So?" She leaned back and held my gaze. "We can't be bound to more than one person? You're my best friend, Lindsey. I won't let you go through it alone."

I felt tears sting my eyes. "Thanks, Kayla. But I'll figure this out. If I can't, I'm not worthy of being a Dark Guardian. I want to be a guardian almost as much as I want to figure out who is truly my destiny."

Before I left, I asked Kayla to explain to Connor where I was and that I knew what I was doing so he wouldn't worry or come after me. Knowing Connor, it probably wouldn't stop him from doing either of those things, but I figured it was worth a try.

Rafe was leaning against the porch post when I slipped outside, and I was hit with the reality of what I was doing.

I was leaving with him. I was going to be alone with him. I was surprised by how desperately I wanted that. I could feel his gaze assessing me, but I was also acutely aware that his usually hard-to-read expression had shifted into one of obvious pleasure. In spite of the dangers that we might face—both in the wilderness and to our hearts— he was glad for my company. I felt an incredible warmth flow through me when he took my hand, threading his strong fingers through mine. I was amazed by how right it felt. Silently, I followed him away from the small village at the edge of the park to where he'd parked his bike, far enough away that no one would hear it.

I climbed on behind Rafe, adjusted my backpack so it was more comfortable, and slid my arms around him, welcoming the strength and warmth that was Rafe.

"Are you sure about this, Lindsey?" he asked, and I knew that he was aware I was taking this journey for a number of reasons—not simply to find the hidden lab.

"Absolutely."

"You know that when Connor gets back and discovers you're gone, he's going to come after you."

"But he can't be mad at me, Rafe. The truth is . . . I'm just following his suggestion."

He released a dark laugh. "Oh, he'll be furious. Count on it."

The bike roared to life. I tightened my hold on Rafe as we took off. A strange sensation skittered through me, and I glanced back over my shoulder. Although I didn't see anything, I couldn't shake the feeling we were being watched.

We rode through the morning and all day long in the thick and verdant forest. We stopped once to quickly eat some sandwiches that Rafe had packed. We didn't talk. Maybe it was the sense of doing something we weren't supposed to that kept us quiet—or maybe we feared being overheard. Maybe we just had nothing to say as the enormity of what we were doing began to sink in. Danger was bound to be involved, and bringing me along was probably not Rafe's smartest move. On the other hand, I didn't think going alone would have been too smart, either.

Heavy darkness had descended before we finally came to a stop for the night. Rafe held me close until my legs adjusted to standing again.

"How long before my legs adapt to riding for such long hours?" I asked.

"Hopefully never. I like holding you."

Relaxing against him, I enjoyed the feel of his arms around me. Burying my nose against his chest, I inhaled the scent that was unique to him. *No matter how this trip ends*, I thought, *I'd never forget his scent*.

"I don't think we should set up a campfire," Rafe said, his chest rumbling with his words. "We have no idea how close anyone might be."

"Do you think we're being followed?"

"I don't know, but I wouldn't put it past those mercenaries that Dallas told us about."

"Do you think they killed him?"

"That's my guess. They might have hung around to
see how we reacted."

"Bastards." Reluctantly, I pulled away from Rafe,
took a small penlight out of my pocket, and scouted the
area. I located a log, sat on it, and turned off the light. I
struggled out of my backpack, wondering how I could be
so tired when all I'd done was ride a bike all day. Every
one of my muscles and bones ached.

We had more moonlight tonight, and I watched as
his silhouette approached and sat beside me. I located the
front pocket on my pack and unzipped it. "I have some
protein bars and a couple of apples."

"Guess that'll work. I can take you back tonight if
you've changed your mind, but once we have two days
behind us—"

"I don't want to go back." I held out a protein bar
and he took it. I grabbed a bottle of water from a side
pocket.

"Tomorrow we'll be close enough to one of our lairs.
We can replenish supplies, sleep in a protected area,"
Rafe said.

We Shifters had set up hidden lairs all over the forest.

We stored food, extra clothes, and any other essentials we thought someone might need if separated from the pack, hurt, or in trouble. The government might technically own the forest, but we viewed it as ours. Some of our ancestors had come over on the *Mayflower*. It was when they'd begun burning them as witches in Salem that we'd taken up residence in this wilderness. It had been designated as a national forest for only about a hundred years, but it had been our home for much longer.

Even in the darkness I was comfortable here.

"Are you supposed to do anything if you find the lab?" I asked. "You know—destroy it, kill everyone within it?"

"Just report its location to Lucas. Then we'll decide how to handle it."

"I hope I've had my first shift by then. I'll be more effective as a wolf."

"I don't know if we can wait that long."

A huff of self-conscious laughter escaped me. "You make it sound like it's so far off, and I'm sitting here thinking that it's rushing at me too fast."

"Most of us are excited about our first transformation." He trailed his finger along my bare arm, and I shivered. "Why aren't you?"

Was he pushing me to admit what I was feeling?

"Can you read my mind?" I asked.

"When I'm in wolf form."

"And when you're not?"

"Sometimes I'll catch a thought."

Was it significant that he could read my thoughts when he wasn't in wolf form—when Connor couldn't?

I pushed myself to my feet. "I don't understand. I thought there was supposed to be one person for each of us, that our instincts recognized the one who was our destiny. I feel like an aberration. I didn't think it was supposed to be this confusing."

"What are you confused by?"

I spun around. "God, Rafe, if you can truly read my mind, you must already know."

"I try not to intrude on your thoughts. Are you giving me permission—"

"No!" I needed my thoughts to stay mine until I figured things out.

"What did you feel when I kissed you?" Rafe asked. I watched his shadowy form lengthen as he came to his feet.

"It was more intense than anything I'd ever experienced. But it could have just been the emotions of the day . . . we were both reacting to them."

"Then let me kiss you again. We'll see how it goes." His voice was low, soothing, almost hypnotic.

"It wouldn't be fair to Connor."

"Are all your doubts fair to him? Things are different for the males among us. During your first transformation, if your mate is with you, if you've chosen him for that moment, he'll bond with you. It'll be permanent. We mate for life. If you change your mind, you can walk away. *We can't.* And if you walk to me afterward, I'll always know that he was there for you during your first time—I'll never have that experience with you."

"But I'll have other transform—"

"It's never like the first time, when everything within us, everything that we are, everything that we will become—it all achieves maturity. A butterfly emerging from its cocoon will always be a butterfly afterward, but that moment of awe when it first spreads its wings—this only happens once. That's the reason the bond forms so strongly with the female's first transformation. She'll never again experience that moment of wonder, and the male—*her* male—wants to experience it with her."

I'd always known the first transformation was profound, but no one had ever explained it like that before.

I didn't know what to say. I thought, *All this shouldn't be a surprise to me.* I'd always known what I was, what the first transformation was—but just like sex, it wasn't anything my mom had ever truly discussed with me. It was an important part of my journey into adulthood, and no one had given me a road map.

144

Suddenly Rafe was closer to me. I could feel the warmth radiating off his body. I wanted to snuggle up against him.

"Why did you come with me if you didn't want to experience what it was for us to be together?" he asked.

I didn't answer him with words. Instead, I reached up and cradled his face between my hands. I could feel the stubble on his jaw. I could feel the slight breeze teasing his long, black hair across my fingers. I could sense his gaze on mine. I was acutely aware of the stillness of him as he waited for me to make my decision.

Forgive me, Connor.

I rose up on my toes to issue my invitation with a soft, and I hoped sexy, voice. "Kiss me."

His low, victorious growl echoed between us and then he was kissing me passionately. And just like the first kiss, this one took my breath. Tonight there wasn't the adrenaline spike of a near-death experience or the heady rush of him having saved my life. But the fire was still there, all-consuming, just like in my dreams. And just like the first kiss, it was overwhelming—it was almost too much.

I pulled back first. I no longer questioned whether lust alone was involved here. Finally I felt that soul-deep connection I'd heard about. I was in trouble. Big trouble.

Lowering my heels back to the ground, I nestled my

cheek into the crook of his shoulder, welcoming his arms as they came around me.

"Are you okay?" he asked.

"I've decided that's the stupidest question on earth."

"So you're not okay."

"I don't know, Rafe. Things just got a lot more complicated."

"I won't say I'm glad, but I'm definitely not disappointed either. At least there's a chance you could choose me."

And what would that do to Connor?

"We need to get some sleep," he said then, and I wondered if he felt a need to fill the silence that was stretching between us. "Share my sleeping bag with me."

Great! I hadn't thought to pack a sleeping bag.

"I can't," I said with a measure of regret. But I knew there were some lines that, once I crossed them, I would never be able to go back.

"You're worrying about Connor again."

"Of course I'm worrying about him. Rafe, he's been part of my life my entire life. Until this summer, neither of us questioned, neither of us doubted . . . and now, I just don't know. Falling in love should be the easiest thing in the world, but it's not."

And that's what made this so complicated: I thought I was falling in love with Rafe. Not just because of the wonderful kisses—it was the fact that he could bare his heart and soul so openly with me. He was strong and good. He cared for me. He knew what he wanted and he went after it. He didn't settle.

Tenderly, he touched my cheek. "I didn't mean to make things harder for you."

"Didn't you?"

"Not intentionally. I wish it were easier, for both of us. But I didn't want to give up if there was a chance we could be together. And if there wasn't a chance, I needed to know that. You did, too."

"I know. I'm not angry. I'm just . . . suddenly very tired."

"I know you didn't bring a sleeping bag," he said. "I promise we'll just sleep."

He didn't wait for my answer, but simply moved to grab his sleeping bag from the back of his bike where it was secured. Although I felt immensely guilty, I couldn't deny the comforting anticipation of curling up beside him, sleeping in his arms. I'd never even thought about lying in Connor's arms. But I knew that it would seem natural with Connor, too. I'd never questioned that he would always be there for me. Now I was worried that I might not be there for him.

I watched as Rafe rolled out the sleeping bag. Crouching, he reached up and threaded his fingers through mine, giving a slight tug. I knelt and stretched out on the sleeping bag. In the next heartbeat he was lying on his back beside me, tucking me into the curve of his side. I could feel the strength in his hold, the firmness in his muscles. I rested my cheek in the nook of his shoulder and listened to the steady pounding of his heart. I thought I should say something, but it seemed that any words I uttered would be insignificant when compared with this moment. He'd promised we would only sleep, but lying this close to him, I found myself wishing for more. I longed for another kiss. I yearned to feel the touch of his fingers on my skin. I wanted that intimacy with a fierceness I'd never experienced before.

Rafe shifted, curling himself around me until I was absorbed in the cocoon of his warmth. I wanted to resist. Instead I relaxed until I fit against him, my body molded to his.

I'd thought we were going in search of the most dangerous thing in the forest. I'd been wrong. Right that moment, the most dangerous thing I could face had his arms wrapped around me—and I'd never felt so remarkably safe.

TWELVE

The next morning, I awoke to find myself still snuggled against Rafe. He'd held me all night, and I didn't want to leave the comfort of his arms. I didn't remember ever sleeping as deeply, even when I was in a bed rather than on the forest floor. As a result, my dreams had been incredibly vivid and disturbingly real. They'd all revolved around Rafe kissing me until my toes curled—which didn't take much time at all. I'd had one awful dream in which he and Connor had fought over me. As far as I knew, that had never happened in the modern era, but apparently it had been quite common among Shifters in ancient times. Sometimes I was amazed that our species hadn't become extinct.

I burrowed my face into the curve of his shoulder, wondering if he was an early riser and what kind of mood he might wake up in. As for me, I couldn't believe how rested I felt.

It was his kiss near my temple that alerted me: He was awake. His lips were soft and warm, and I wanted to bring them down to mine and kiss him deeply, but I was afraid to indulge my wishes until I was sure of my feelings. I couldn't deny that they were growing, but would they exceed the affection I felt for Connor? Had they already surpassed those feelings? Was it even possible to measure what the heart felt?

I tilted my head back and met Rafe's warm, brown gaze. Before I could say *good morning*, he was kissing me, sweeping away my doubts and my guilt. For a few moments, lost in the wonder of his mouth moving over mine, I was on vacation, with no worries, no stress, no pressing dangers. I relaxed into him and felt his muscles bunching and relaxing as I skimmed my fingers over his shoulders and back. He was so strong, so powerful. I wanted this, I wanted the surety he exhibited, I wanted to know—to know *deep down*—that he was the one. But several hours in his company couldn't erase the lifetime I'd spent with Connor as the male meant for me.

Regretfully, I pulled back. His gaze touched on each

aspect of my face—my chin, my lips, my nose, my eyes, my forehead—as if he wished to continue kissing them all.

"Too early for spontaneous kisses?" he asked quietly.

I nodded. He gave me a wry grin. I stroked the corner of his mouth. "I'm sorry."

"Don't be, Lindsey. I'm patient. The moon isn't."

With that reminder, he rolled out of the sleeping bag. I immediately mourned his absence. Shaking off this yearning, I sat up, reached for my backpack, and removed my hairbrush. After unbraiding my hair, I worked the brush through it.

Rafe crouched in front of me and set down a package of six chocolate-covered doughnuts.

"Oh, my favorites," I said excitedly.

"I know."

I looked up at him. "How did you know?"

"You're a chocolate fiend." Reaching out, he tugged playfully on my hair. "Wear it loose today."

"It'll be a tangled mess by tonight."

"I'll comb it out."

"Have you ever fought the tangles in windblown hair? It's a battle you'll want to avoid. Sorry. I'll wear it down when we go to bed tonight."

He gave me a sexy grin. "That'll work."

After a hastily eaten breakfast, we packed up and I positioned myself behind Rafe on the bike. "Can you tap into my dreams like you do my thoughts?" I asked.

He gave me a sideways look and winked. "Only if I'm awake."

Before I could ask if he had slept last night—I had to know if he'd seen my dreams—he'd turned on the engine and we were flying through the forest again.

It wasn't as bright as it had been the day before. If it rained, we probably would have to travel by foot because the bike might get stuck in the mud—or we'd have to wait until everything dried up again. I wasn't sure which option would cost us less precious time.

As we traveled farther north, the blackening clouds seemed an ominous sign. Even if all we were going to do was discover the location of the lab and report back, we were at risk of being captured. If they believed we were Shifters, they'd do experiments on us. No law would protect us, because no law acknowledged our existence, except for our own. Maybe PETA would step in and rant about cruelty to animals—but we weren't really "animals" in that sense. Nor were we completely human. I couldn't help but wonder once again if the time had come for us to step out of the woods, so to speak.

About an hour before dusk, we ran out of gas. Rafe had made adjustments to his bike so it would go farther than most on a tank of gas, and I thought maybe the tank was larger as well. But even the best mechanic can't foresee all possible mishaps, especially in a swath of wilderness this large. He didn't seem at all bothered by our predicament, probably because he knew we were near one of our lairs, where we had provisions stored.

I didn't mind walking. I was accustomed to hiking far and wide. Part of me wanted to walk fast and part of me wanted to take my time. Our lairs were usually built inside a mountain or a hill. They provided some comfort. Tonight Rafe and I would be alone in one. Would I be strong enough to resist the offer of another kiss? Would we sleep in each other's arms again? And knowing that we were hidden away and completely safe, would we find the strength to resist temptation?

I glanced around at the familiar wilderness that suddenly felt foreign, violated. "What if they've set traps for us? They must know that if someone told us about a lab, we'd come searching for it."

"Then let's hope I fall into it and not you," Rafe said. "I can shift and heal. You, I'd have to somehow take back to civilization."

"You're anticipating that we would escape from the trap. What if we get hauled to their lab?"

Reaching out, he softly touched my cheek. "I won't let anything happen to you, Lindsey."

I thought about his fight with the cougar. But Bio-Chrome was another kind of animal altogether.

"How could they build a lab so near the national forest without anyone noticing?" I asked.

"It's a sparsely populated area, and we can't patrol all of it all the time. I've heard about drug cartels growing their poppies and marijuana plants on government land—*inside* a national forest—right beneath the noses of rangers. It can't all be watched."

"I guess it would lose its appeal if we set up surveillance cameras everywhere."

He glanced over at me and grinned. "Absolutely. No private moments for making out."

His gaze dropped to my lips, which began to tingle, and I knew he was thinking about kissing me again. It was so tempting. I needed to think about something else. "So who do you think killed Dallas? Could it have been one of us? Someone who didn't trust him? Or could it have been random?"

"Those are always possibilities, but I think it's more likely that it was someone hired by Bio-Chrome. Dallas was going to betray them. And they're not making a big fuss about coming after us because they want to keep our existence quiet. They're trying to lay low, to avoid involving the authorities, until they have a formula or whatever they think they can create to duplicate our abilities."

"What if we can't stop them?"

"We'll stop them." Nonchalantly, he continued pushing

the bike up an incline and through a crevice in the low-rising mountain.

He sounded so sure. He made me believe him, made me believe that everything was going to be all right. In such a short time, I was coming to know him so much better that more than just his kisses impressed me. He was a natural leader. We followed a winding path until we came to a spot where water babbled over small rock outcroppings and disappeared into an underground spring. I'd been here before; this was one of our lairs.

"Hold the bike," Rafe ordered.

I watched as his muscles flexed when he rolled the large boulder aside. It was nearly nightfall as I slipped into the cool, dark cavern. As Rafe pushed his motorbike inside, I glanced around, trying to give my eyes a chance to adjust. I wanted to pretend we were in a magical place where the real world couldn't interfere. When Rafe came up behind me, wrapped his arms around my waist, and kissed the nape of my neck, I twisted around and welcomed him. I knew I should object, but there was something about being in the dark that called to the wildness in me, just as he did. He trailed his mouth over the curve of my neck. Pleasure tiptoed along my spine, and I felt like a cat stretching in the sun. But even in the happy darkness with Rafe, I couldn't help but think of Connor. Guilt hammered at me, and I stepped out of his embrace before his lips could settle again on mine.

A dim light suddenly illuminated the cave. I spun around, curious, and watched Rafe walk away from the battery-powered lantern he'd turned on. Reaching up, he dropped a black curtain over the entranceway, shutting out the world.

Rafe faced me, his gaze holding mine, and I could see in his eyes that he wanted me to give him more than I was ready to give. He wanted me to pretend that in this world there were only the two of us. I couldn't deny that it was tempting. He'd come to me a few minutes ago. Now it was my turn to go to him. Before the night was over, I thought I probably would. How could I resist?

I wasn't sure whether he read my mind or my face revealed how much I wanted him, but he gave me a slow, lazy smile, and his gaze grew warmer. He'd said he was patient, but even more important, he was understanding.

He walked over to a large plastic container and reached inside, then tossed me a can of Vienna sausages. Not my favorite, but I was hungry enough that I didn't complain as I sat on the cool, hard ground. We stocked these places for emergencies. What was going on now certainly qualified.

"How do we know we're headed in the right direction?" I asked.

Sitting on one of the crates that housed supplies, Rafe was enjoying his own can of sausages. "Dallas said the lab is in the northeast corner, so I know the direction is right. I'm hoping as we get nearer to the Bio-Chrome people, I'll pick up their scents."

"That would be easier if you could travel in wolf form."

Shrugging, he grinned. "Easier, but not as much fun."

"Yeah, I'm a real barrel of laughs."

"You stop me from getting lonely."

I studied him for a minute, thinking back to when I knew him in school. "You always struck me as a loner."

"It was easier that way."

"What do you mean, exactly?" I asked.

He plucked a sausage out of the can and chewed on it for a while. "You asked the other night if it's about me wanting things I can't have."

"I was just . . . I don't know. I shouldn't have said that."

"No, you were right. When I was growing up, I wanted parents who went to the school on open-house night and gave a damn about my school projects. I wanted a father who would toss me a football instead of beating the crap out of me. When I became friends with someone, I'd see a lot of things that I wanted, things I knew I'd never have. Not material things, not gadgets, but things like eating supper at a table with all the family there."

My chest tightened until I felt a painful knot in its center. I'd known that he hadn't grown up in my world, but I'd never realized the full extent of our differences.

"You were the only one who never stared at me when I came to school with bruises or a black eye," he said quietly.

"My parents always told me not to stare." Although I seemed to have forgotten my manners, because lately I was staring at Rafe a lot. Now, as he was talking about his past, I wanted to do more than just watch him. I wanted to hold him, comfort him. "Your dad did that to you, didn't he? He beat you."

"Yeah. He spent a lot of his time drunk. I could never please him when he was like that. He used to take his fists to me. Sometimes I'd tell people I got into a fight. It was easier to pretend to be a bully than to let people know the truth: My dad hated my guts."

"No!" I protested vehemently. "He was sick. No one could hate you, Rafe."

Giving me a wry grin, he shook his head. "You know, when I was younger, I couldn't wait until my first trans-formation, because then I'd have the ability to heal faster. People wouldn't know how often he beat me. Then he died in that car accident and it was all moot. I was glad he was dead." He paused. "Does that part of me frighten you?"

I held his gaze. "No, I never liked him either. He scared me."

Rafe snapped to attention. "Did he do something to

scare you? Did he ever hurt you?"

"No way. My dad would have taken him down if he did. He just looked so mean. He was always scowling, like he was mad at the world."

"I'd never hurt you, Lindsey. I'm not like my dad."

"I know." And I did. Yes, Rafe scared me. But it was because of what I felt for him—something I'd never felt for anyone else. And tonight we'd be in this small cavern, snuggling against each other. Maybe we'd even kiss again. I'd spent a lot of time today thinking about what might happen tonight.

I got up and put the empty can into a plastic bag that we'd take with us. We were always careful not to trash our environment. "I'm going to the pool."

Rafe looked at me intently, as though he was wondering if I was inviting him along. I wasn't. I needed some time alone to let my nerves settle. I knew nothing would happen here that I didn't want to happen. The problem was that I wasn't exactly sure what I *did* want to happen.

I went over to a plastic crate where we stored extra clothes. I found a small pair of drawstring cotton pants and a long-sleeved cotton shirt that would hug my sleek body; my curves weren't nearly as pronounced as Brittany's. I bundled up everything I needed, including a big, square flashlight that shone a wide beam, and headed toward the back of the cavern. The passageway narrowed, and the light bounced off the walls. We'd created this haven inside the mountain, and because we kept the entrance blocked, I wasn't afraid to be here by myself.

Around the corner, the passageway opened up into another cavern where the underground stream emptied into a pool. I knelt at the water's edge and flicked off the flashlight. Giving my eyes a moment to adjust, it wasn't long before I was able to see tiny fluorescent creatures moving through the stream. But the pool was completely clear. The constant supply of fresh water kept algae—and anything else that might have made me shudder—from growing.

Turning the light back on, I dipped a cloth into the water and began wiping the gritty dirt from my face. I imagined Rafe trailing kisses all over it. Even though the air surrounding me carried a definite chill, I suddenly grew hot. I stripped off my clothes and dove in. It wasn't the first time I'd gone swimming here. The water was cold as usual, but it felt good.

I washed my hair and my body. Getting rid of two days of grit was exhilarating—until I climbed out of the pool and chill bumps erupted over my skin. Grabbing a towel, I briskly dried off and got dressed. I towel-dried my hair as much as possible before combing it out. I considered braiding it as usual, but Rafe had asked me not to, and I had this insane urge to make him smile and to feel his fingers running through my loose hair.

I glanced toward the passageway, wondering exactly what was waiting for me on the other side. Surely we would sleep in each other's arms again. Tingles of anticipation cascaded through me. I wanted to be with him— almost desperately. I had never experienced that level of feeling with Connor: pure desire. Until I'd met Kayla, Connor had been my best friend, the one I did everything with. He was comfortable, but Rafe was . . . exciting.

I gathered everything together and strolled as calmly as I could through the passage. As I neared the entrance I heard voices.

Apparently we were no longer alone.

I immediately recognized one of the voices, and I realized with regret that I wouldn't be sleeping with Rafe tonight. As a matter of fact, he might never hold me in his arms again.

Halting at the entrance to the main cavern, I saw Lucas and Connor practically cornering Rafe. Kayla was standing a short distance away, appearing very uncomfortable. I knew she'd witnessed a confrontation between Lucas and his brother—the one who'd betrayed us. Like me, she was well aware that the guys could be very intimidating when their testosterone levels peaked.

"What were you thinking bringing Lindsey with you?"

Connor demanded of Rafe, and my heart slammed against my ribs with the fury I heard in his voice.

"I wanted to come," I answered before Rafe could.

Connor jerked around, his eyes resting on me. I knew him well enough to see that he wasn't surprised by my presence, so Kayla had told him as I'd asked. In some ways, it made things easier, and in others so much harder. I could see in his eyes that he wanted to ask me questions, that he was remembering the fight we never finished. I saw regret . . . and sorrow. At that particular moment I was feeling the same thing. But I was also angry; Rafe was being blamed for my actions.

"What were you thinking?" Connor asked fiercely.

"Don't talk to her like that," Rafe said. His voice was deeper than usual and carried the hint of a threat.

"It's okay, Rafe," I said, trying to calm the situation. "Everyone's emotions are high right now."

Since they'd caught up with us so quickly, I assumed they'd traveled in wolf form. We had plenty of extra clothes here for emergencies like this, and they were all dressed now, Kayla wearing loose pants similar to the ones I was wearing.

"I thought I could help," I told Connor.

"How? If you get hurt—"

"I didn't get hurt."

"You didn't get permission either," Lucas said, and it

irritated me that he was siding with Connor.

"Uh, you're not the boss of me." I knew that sounded juvenile, but I didn't appreciate the accusation.

"Actually I am. 'Pack leader' is another name for 'boss.'"

"If you're going to get mad at someone, get mad at me," Rafe insisted. "I knew better and I brought her anyway."

"And why exactly did you bring her?" Connor asked.

"You know why," Rafe said, and I realized he was as angry as Connor.

Connor lunged for him. I heard the sickening thud of a fist hitting flesh and bone as they both went down. I screamed, "Stop it! Both of you stop it!"

Only they didn't. They just kept pounding into each other. It wasn't the way we fought. I looked at Lucas, who was standing with his arms crossed over his chest as though he was waiting for a bus to arrive. "Do something!" I shouted at him.

He shifted his hard gaze over to me. "What do you suggest?"

I released a harsh curse and jumped into the fray, trying to get their attention. "Guys! Conn—"

Pain ricocheted along my cheek and into my eye. I shrieked and stumbled backward.

"*Shit!* You hit her!" Rafe said, suddenly kneeling

beside me. His face was a bruised and bloody mess, and I thought about all the beatings he'd taken from his father. I reached up to touch his darkening cheek.

"I didn't hit her. You did," Connor said, crouching on the other side of me, touching my cheek with a tenderness that was in direct contrast to what he'd been doing just a few seconds ago.

I looked at him. He'd taken the brunt of the punches. One of his eyes was almost swollen shut. I touched the mottled flesh. He winced, and I couldn't help myself. I started to cry.

He took me into the circle of his arms and held me close, which just made me cry harder. "I don't know, Connor. I just don't know."

He rocked me side to side. "It's okay. I know."

I heard scraping along the ground as Rafe got up.

"I'm going outside to heal," he said, his voice flat, devoid of emotion. I couldn't tell what he was thinking.

I didn't want him to leave—but at the same time, was it fair to ask him to stay? I worked my way out of Connor's embrace and swiped at my tears. "You should go heal, too." I felt so stupid for losing it in front of everyone. I was so confused. How could I love two guys at once?

He placed a light kiss on my bruise. "Be here when I get back."

I didn't know where exactly he thought I was going to go, and then I realized he was asking me to be there *for him.* Out of habit, I nodded.

He stood, but instead of going outside like Rafe had, he went into the passageway where the pool was.

Kayla knelt beside me. "I think you're going to have a beauty of a black eye."

"It doesn't matter." I'd stopped them from killing each other. That was the only thing I considered important.

"I take it you're not any closer to figuring things out."

I shook my head. "If at all possible, I'm just more confused. So what happened with the birdwatchers?"

"Zander took them out. I wanted to be here in case, you know, you needed some support."

I gave her a grateful smile. "I'm glad you're here, but I really need to talk with Connor." I shoved myself to my feet and met Lucas's gaze. "How long do you think the healing will take?"

"A few minutes."

"Did Connor ask you to reassign Rafe?"

His face was an unreadable mask—and ironically, this gave me the answer.

"So moving Daniel to our team wasn't about finding someone for Brittany."

"It was. It just wasn't the only reason."

I had a brief moment of wondering how things were going with Brittany, before I grabbed my flashlight and strode into the passageway. I found Connor sitting at the edge of the pool, fully clothed. A quick sweep of the light revealed that he no longer had any injuries. With a sigh I settled down beside him and stared at the pool of water, trying to figure out where I should go from here.

"I'm sorr—" we both started at the same time. Then we each released a self-conscious laugh.

I longed for the days when we were completely comfortable with each other, when we both knew what we wanted. Or thought we did.

"You told me to go out with him," I said quietly.

"I didn't mean it. I mean, I was upset. But if I had meant it, I would have been talking about going to a movie for a couple of hours, not trekking through the woods for days—and certainly not putting your life at risk."

"I'm a Dark Guardian. That's my job."

"You're a novice. You can't heal like we do. You can't transform, and you can't escape as easily if there's danger."

"You're not mad about the danger," I said softly.

"Do you want to be with him? I mean, are you going to choose him?"

"I don't know, Connor. But he's not the only reason I'm here. I asked to come because I wanted to help. Maybe because we found Dallas, and I feel partly responsible for his death."

Connor looked shocked by my words. "It's not your fault."

"In a way it is, because of the whole blackberries

incident—but whatever. I wanted to feel useful; I wanted to take an active part in making Bio-Chrome pay. I didn't want to guide birdwatchers. It's not the first time I've opted for adventure over the ordinary."

Some of Connor's anger dissipated, and his mouth twitched toward a smile. I knew he was remembering a dozen occasions when I'd convinced him to do something that eventually got us into trouble. I didn't always think through to the ramifications of my choices, but we'd always had fun.

Gently, he tucked my hair behind my ear. "Do you . . . do you love him?"

He wouldn't say Rafe's name, as though if we talked about him in the abstract, he wouldn't be significant. I told him the truth.

"I don't know. I didn't expect it to be this hard. Kayla said she felt an instant connection with Lucas, and Brittany doesn't feel a soul-deep connection with anyone. I care about both you and Rafe. I don't want to hurt either one of you, and I worry that I'll make the wrong decision."

"Maybe you need to stop worrying about it. Just"— he sighed—"let us figure it out."

By us, I knew he meant him and Rafe. I scoffed. "Yeah, that's gonna work."

"I was winning," he said petulantly.

It was such a guy thing to say.

"I thought you were the one who wanted us to be more civilized," I reminded him.

"Hey, I was civilized. I didn't shift."

Any other time, I would have laughed. Instead, leaning over, I put my head on his shoulder. "I'm sorry I don't know the answer."

"Yeah. Me, too."

He put his arm around me and we sat there for a while, just absorbing the feel of each other. We were always like this. We were each other's rock. But did it make us each other's destiny?

After a while, we got up and walked back into the main part of the cavern. It didn't even register with me that we were holding hands—until I saw Rafe leaning against a wall and his gaze dipped to where our hands were joined. A storm of emotions passed through his eyes.

"I'll keep watch tonight," he said tersely, and he strode out of the cavern before anyone could respond.

I wanted to go after him, but Connor squeezed my hand. Was it a silent plea to stay with him, or a reminder that we'd been together forever? How loyal was I supposed to be while I figured things out?

"I'll fix us a place to sleep," he said quietly.

I glanced over to where Connor was laying out a sleeping bag on the opposite side of the cavern from where Kayla was preparing one for her and Lucas. I rubbed my hands up and down my arms. I'd never slept beside Connor. If he was truly my destined mate, shouldn't I be excited about it instead of worrying that it might be awkward? And could I sleep beside him tonight, knowing that I'd slept beside Rafe last night?

When everything was ready, he took my hand and led me over to the pallet. It took us a while to get settled. I bumped his chin with my head. He chuckled, told me to relax. I shifted around until my back was to him and he was spooned around me. His arm came around me and I threaded my fingers through his. He smelled different than Rafe. He felt different than Rafe.

Lucas turned out the lantern and plunged us into darkness. I could hear him and Kayla talking low, like lovers do.

"This doesn't feel right, Connor," I whispered.

"Okay, roll over and put your head on my shoulder."

"No, that's not what I meant. Lying here with you . . . If you were the one guarding us tonight, would you want me here, sleeping beside Rafe?"

"It's not the same, Lindsey. Until you decide otherwise, you're mine. I have a symbol representing your name inked on my shoulder."

"So does he," I said quietly.

I felt him tense, right before he cursed. The ink was never done lightly, and Connor knew it.

"He didn't declare for you in front of everyone. I did."

"It's not about who observes more traditions. It's about our hearts."

"You've always had mine."

I squeezed my eyes shut. One minute he was understanding, and the next he was making it so difficult by declaring his feelings. I didn't doubt his. I no longer doubted Rafe's. I doubted mine. But how did I explain that?

THIRTEEN

Connor fell asleep. I was pretty sure that Lucas and Kayla had drifted off as well. I, on the other hand, didn't sleep. Not a wink. I kept thinking about Rafe and the storm of emotions in his eyes before he'd walked out. After the fight, I'd consoled Connor. I should have done the same for Rafe. Guilt over what I was beginning to feel for him had kept me from his side. It was totally unfair.

Gingerly, I eased away from Connor. He was fast asleep, dead to the world. I crept toward the cavern's covered opening. Although it was dark, I knew my way around the cavern, and there was nothing for me to trip over. I slipped outside, surprised to discover the sun just starting to lighten the sky.

I glanced around but couldn't see Rafe. He'd said he was going to guard us, but I didn't think we really needed a guard. We were pretty well hidden. I suspected he just wanted to avoid another fight.

A shiver went through me. It was cold out, but there was more to it than just the chill in the air. Something didn't feel right—just like the night we found Dallas. I had a sense that something ominous was lurking around.

I started to go back into the cavern when I heard movement off to the side, from the direction that Rafe and I had originally arrived at the lair. Pressing back against the wall of the mountain, trying to make myself as invisible as possible, I inched stealthily along the path, holding my breath, trying not to make any sort of noise. I wasn't certain what I'd do if I ran into anyone, but I felt like I needed to check it out.

I went around a curve in the pathway and rammed into someone. My heart jumped into my throat, turning my scream into a pitiful squeak. Then, with a rush of relief, I realized it was Rafe. I pressed my hand to my thundering heart. "Oh my God! You scared me. I thought you were Bio-Chrome."

I took a couple of deep breaths, trying to calm my erratic heart. Rafe was all but ignoring me as he pulled his T-shirt down over his head.

"What are you doing?" I asked.

"Getting dressed." He dropped down and began pulling on his hiking boots.

I crouched beside him. "I thought you were going to keep watch."

"Felt a need to run instead."

I knew without asking that he'd shifted in order to do it.

"I thought about not coming back," he said as he jerked on his shoelace and tightly tied it. "But I've never been one for avoiding a situation. If you loved him, why didn't you just say so?"

Him. He was doing the same thing as Connor: not using his name, as though that somehow lessened whatever he was feeling.

"I don't blame you for being mad because I went to him in the cavern. I shouldn't have. Or maybe I should have gone to you as well, given you equal time. I'm sorry I didn't come to you sooner. I'm sorry about a lot of things, but I'm not sorry that you and I have had this time together. You want to hear something crazy? It was Connor's idea."

"Like hell."

"No, really. Right before we found Dallas, we were arguing about you. He said I needed to spend time with you. Now he says he didn't mean it—but we never finished the argument, so I didn't know that. And now I'm just more confused. It's not supposed to be like this—or at least I didn't think it was. I thought it was supposed to be destiny. I thought we were supposed to have this *zing!* and just immediately know who our mates were."

He finally stopped getting dressed. He stared off in the distance, dangling his wrists over his bent knees. "You're going to have choose, Lindsey. And soon."

"I know." I watched the sky turn the brilliant, deep blue of dawn. "Maybe Brittany's right, and we should just go through it by ourselves, then fall in love on our own timetable and not on the moon's."

He wrapped several strands of my hair around his fingers and gave a light tug. I shifted my gaze over to his. The intensity of emotion in his eyes stole my breath.

"No matter what you decide," he said quietly, "it won't change what I feel for you. I wish it hadn't hit me like a thunderbolt this summer. I wish it had happened sooner. I wish I'd had more time to . . . I don't know . . . date you. Let you get to know me better. I know Connor has the advantage because he's got years of knowing you on his side." He leaned in and very tenderly pressed his lips to my bruised eye. "I'm sorry for that. I never meant for you to get hurt."

I wanted to kiss him in return. Instead I simply

squeezed his hand. "The others are probably up now, wondering where we are."

"Yeah, we should probably go." He came to his feet and pulled me to mine.

I started walking back the way I'd come. "How close—"

Rafe drew me back and put his finger to my lips to silence me. "Do you hear that? Smell that?" he whispered after a second.

"No, what?"

"A lot of feet. People. And the smell of dogs. Wait here."

I hadn't followed a single order yet on this trip, and I wasn't about to start now. Trailing behind him, I followed him to the edge of the curve in the rock wall. He peered around it.

I tried to look, too.

He shoved me back against the wall, and I could see in his eyes that something bad was waiting around the bend. "It's Mason. He has a couple of guys with him. They have to be the mercenaries Dallas mentioned. And they've got dogs—Rottweilers. Those things could easily tear out a person's throat."

"What? No! We have to warn the others."

He started tearing off his clothes. "It's too late, Lindsey. They're at the cave. I'm going to shift so I can go

175

higher, look down, and assess the situation. You need to get far away, before the dogs pick up on your scent."

"Absolutely not! I have to do something."

He grabbed my arms and shook me. "If the others are captured, we're going to have to rescue them. Please, just start running. I'll catch up to you. I promise."

I wrenched myself free of his hold and peered around the corner.

"Lindsey—"

"Shh!"

I could see the two massive dogs growling and barking, straining their leashes. I recognized one of the handlers as the bald guy I'd seen at the Sly Fox that night when we first met Dallas. He looked even meaner than I remembered.

My heart beat erratically as I saw Kayla, Lucas, and Connor—with their hands tied behind their backs—being dragged out of the cavern by guys who looked like they ate nails for breakfast and carried around fifty-pound weights for fun. With his arms crossed over his chest, Mason greeted them. "Well, we meet again."

His brown hair fell over his brow. I remembered that he had pretty green eyes—eyes that we couldn't trust. How could he want to hurt us?

Kayla squared her shoulders. "Mason, what are you doing here?"

"Looking for you, of course," Mason said. "We have

some unfinished business."

Oh, God. I slipped back around the rocky outcropping so I could no longer see them. Squeezing my eyes shut, I pressed my back against the wall of the mountain and tried to block out the images of what I'd seen. I was terrified for them. What was Mason going to do to them? I tried to grab onto some positive thought. I didn't think Mason realized that Kayla was one of us. That could save her. But Lucas—Mason had suspicions about him. What did he think about Connor?

I pounded my fist against the hard surface. How had this happened? Had Dallas been leading us into a trap all along? I felt nauseous and thought I was going to be sick.

"Lindsey, we have to go. The dogs are distracted now, but pretty soon they'll catch our scent."

Rafe was right. Although it felt cowardly to leave, I knew we had to run now so we would be free to help them escape. I didn't wait for Rafe to finish undressing and shift. I just turned on my heel and began racing away as fast as I could. The whole time, though, doubts spurred me on.

How had they found us? Where had Rafe truly gone? Did he want to be rid of Connor so badly that he'd told Mason where to find him?

Kayla had trusted Mason. She'd liked him. And he'd used her.

Had I misjudged Rafe? Was he like his father? Would he hurt those he loved? Did he love me?

* * *

I didn't know how far to run. Like all Shifters, I was blessed with endurance beyond what humans can fathom. And like all sherpas, I had a great sense of direction, so I knew I wasn't going to get lost. I just wanted to get beyond the scent of the dogs. I scrambled over rough terrain, fell, scraped my knee, and cursed myself for leaving a blood trail. I hit a stream and waded through it for a while, the cold water numbing my cuts. Then I crossed over to the other side and backtracked. With any luck, if the dogs did come after me, they would become confused and lose track of my scent.

Or they'd chase Rafe instead. The scent of a wolf would probably attract them much more readily than my scent. Dropping to the ground, trembling from exhaustion, fear, and fury, I leaned against a tree and fought not to cry as the truth hit me hard.

Rafe hadn't shifted so he could get into a better position to observe. He'd shifted because he was planning to draw the dogs away from me. I knew it as surely as I knew my name.

How could I have doubted his loyalty? *Oh, God—I hope he was too busy to tap into my thoughts*. Of course, they were so confused lately that I wasn't sure anyone could make sense of them anyway. One minute I was worried about Connor; the next, my concern was for Rafe.

But my anxiety for Connor was about his safety alone. Whenever I thought about Rafe, the thoughts were more intense, filled with more dread—as though if something bad happened to him, it would happen to a part of me as well.

During the late afternoon, it occurred to me that when I'd wiped out my scent for the dogs, I might have prevented Rafe from finding me, too.

Great! I muttered inwardly. Now what? Should I try to return to the park entrance and alert the park rangers? Should I go back home and tell my dad, who had influence with the governor? These options meant opening up this struggle to the entire community of Shifters. And if we went into full-scale attack mode, there was a good chance that all our secrets would be revealed to the community at large—to the world. But if I did nothing or tried to do something by myself . . . If I failed . . .

I heard a twig snap and froze.

How long had I been sitting here, not paying attention to my surroundings, not listening for the sound of frenzied barking or the tread of heavy boots? Luckily, I could tell it was just a single being—dog or man, I didn't know. But at least the odds weren't totally against me.

I searched around until I found a good, solid branch that I could use as a weapon. I circled the large trunk of the tree and took up a position for attack in the opposite direction from where I'd heard the noise. If the person or whatever was coming this way, he—or it—would have to walk past me, and then *bam*! I'd knock him out and take my own prisoner. Not that I thought Mason would do any negotiating, but I'd take whatever small victory I could.

My mouth grew dry and my palms sweaty. My chest ached with a tightness as I tried not to breathe, not to make any movements that could be detected. I heard a soft footfall and tightened my grip around the branch.

Someone came into my line of vision. I swung blindly and suddenly found myself tackled to the ground by a heavy body. I'd lost my hold on the club, but I still had fists and started pounding—

"What the hell? Lindsey!"

Rafe grabbed my wrists and held them over my head. I could feel my rapid pulse beating against his thumb. His face was directly above mine, his chocolate-brown gaze homing in on mine.

"Oh my God, Rafe! I thought—" I couldn't say aloud what I thought. That he was dead, or that he would never find me. That the enemy was near. And that the Shifters' world as we knew it was totally destroyed.

"It's okay," he murmured over and over, leaning down to kiss my temple, my forehead, my nose, my chin. "It's okay."

With the comforting weight of his body on top of

mine, I could almost believe him. I could almost believe that everything we'd seen happen earlier had been nothing more than a nightmare. He was real and warm and solid. He was with me, and I felt an overwhelming sense of relief. He released his hold on my wrists, and I reached up to touch the face that had been haunting my dreams. I combed my fingers through his thick hair. Caressing him, being caressed by him—it calmed me, brought order to my world.

All the terror that I'd been feeling was suddenly manageable. And I knew—*knew*—he would figure out a way for us to save our friends.

"So what did you find out?" I asked.

"That their dogs are fast and ferocious."

I laid my palm against his cheek, my heart swelling. "You shifted so you could better draw them away from me."

He dipped his head down and brushed his lips over mine as lightly as a butterfly would land on a petal. We both knew that now wasn't the time for anything more— that whatever feelings we'd been trying to sort out would have to wait. At that moment, I didn't think I could have adored him any more than I already did. No matter what I decided about my future, this moment between us would always be precious, simply because he was putting the welfare of others before our own pleasure.

"What those dogs would have done to me if they caught me—it was nothing compared with what Connor would have done to me if something had happened to you," he said.

He was trying to make light of it, but I knew what he'd risked.

"Has Mason hurt them?"

With a sigh he rolled off me. "Not yet. They're marching them somewhere, hands bound behind their backs."

"So we can rescue them tonight?"

He squinted at the late afternoon sun and rubbed his nose. "We probably could, but I don't think we should. I think we should follow, see where they're going."

"Are you crazy?" I shoved myself to a sitting position. "We can't rescue them soon enough, as far as I'm concerned."

"Just calm down for a minute and think about it, Lindsey. They're going to take them to the lab. This way, we'll know its location because they'll lead us right to it."

I didn't like this plan. I didn't like delaying things. But that didn't mean I couldn't see the wisdom in letting the Bio-Chrome scientists lead us right to the lab.

"So what do we do?" I asked.

"I think we go back to the lair tonight, see what we can salvage. They trashed the place."

"Don't you think they're still watching it?"

"They left someone behind, but I already took care of him."

I didn't want to ask exactly what he'd done. Our very existence was in jeopardy. Any action was justified.

FOURTEEN

To say they'd trashed the place was an understatement. Clothes and food were strewn everywhere. It added insult to injury.

"How did they even know where to find us?" I asked, baffled. No way could Mason have found this place— unless he knew exactly where to look.

"I haven't a clue."

"Someone must have told them."

Rafe spun around and scrutinized me. "You don't think it was me, do you?"

I held his gaze steadily and told him the truth. "No."

He seemed to release a breath he'd been holding. "I

wouldn't have blamed you if you did. I'm supposed to be on watch, and instead I go for a run—and in walks the enemy."

I went over to him and touched his cheek. I may have had doubts earlier, but that had been fear taking over all rational thought. "I know you wouldn't betray us."

He shook his head, and I could see the shame in his eyes. "I should have taken my job more seriously. This is my fault."

"No, Rafe, it's not. Just like Dallas's death isn't mine. We're looking for someone to blame. We can blame Mason and Bio-Chrome."

He nodded with determination. "You're right. I made a mistake, but I can fix it."

I glanced around again. The food had been opened, smashed, stepped on. Even Rafe's bike was toppled on its side. I thought I must have been watching too many undercover cop shows, because I suddenly had this insane idea: If they'd hired mercenaries to track us down . . .

"Could there be some kind of locating device on your bike?" I asked.

"What? When would they have put it there?"

I shrugged. "The clerk at the hotel said someone was looking for Dallas. Maybe whoever it was overheard you talking with Dallas about meeting up."

"I did point my bike out to him. Maybe one of Bio-

Chrome's mercenaries overheard me talking to him and confirmed that I was a Shifter. Damn it." He rushed over to the bike, knelt down, and began probing every nook and cranny. Cursing, he held up a small disk. "This doesn't belong."

He dropped it on the ground and lifted his foot.

"No, wait!"

He lowered his foot. "What are you thinking?"

"If they left someone here, then they must not think they've gotten everyone. Any chance you could attach that to a rabbit or something?"

"Send them on a wild goose chase. I like your thinking." Grinning, he winked at me. "But then, I like everything about you."

I felt the heat flush my face. I liked everything about him, too.

With his brow furrowed and his jaw tensed, he looked around. I knew what he was thinking.

"I'll be fine," I assured him.

He nodded. "I'll be quick."

After he disappeared outside, I sat on an overturned crate and felt the tears sting my eyes at the sight of the destruction. It seemed like an omen for what might happen to all of us Shifters. Bio-Chrome, Mason, his father—they were working to destroy all that we'd built.

And it looked as though they were going to succeed.

Without Rafe there, the cavern that had once served as our refuge seemed incredibly ominous. Every time I heard a noise coming from outside, I froze, barely breathing, poised to fight whoever came for me. The minutes ticked by as slowly as hours.

Absently, I cleaned up the mess, keeping my senses alert to anyone who might be approaching. Sometimes the anger took hold and I threw clothes, blankets, and canned foods into the containers as though *they* were the enemy. Then a deep sadness would well up inside me and I'd take great care to fold the blankets so they wouldn't wrinkle, to line up the remaining cans so the labels were clearly visible to whichever Shifter might make use of this lair after us.

Then I realized that we'd probably have to abandon this site. It was no longer our sanctuary.

I tried really hard not to think about my friends. The pain I felt for them was excruciating. I hurt for Lucas because he was our leader, always looking out for our best interests. For Kayla because she'd only just come into our world, and this was a hell of a welcome. And for Connor because I couldn't imagine him not being in my life.

It didn't help when I picked up a can of Red Bull—Connor's favorite energy drink. Trailing my fingers over it, and thinking that Connor could have it after we rescued them, I decided to put it in my backpack.

When I twisted around to look for it, my gaze fell on a shadow just inside the doorway. I released a small shriek before I realized who it was. Relief swamped me.

"Oh my God, Rafe you made me jump out of my skin," I scolded lightly as I hurried over to him and wound my arms around his neck. "I was so worried. It was taking you so long."

He hugged me to him and held me close. "Sorry, Lindsey. I saw them and decided to follow along for a while, to make sure they're okay. Connor and Lucas are both a little bruised. I figure they put up a fight. And they look mad. Mason is liable to discover that he doesn't like them when they're mad."

I released a small laugh at the image of Connor and Lucas nipping at Mason's heels as they marched, biding their time until they can make him pay. It felt good to smile.

"Also, I had to be a little more careful, catching a rabbit I didn't intend to eat. Took longer than I expected."

I felt like I never wanted him to let me go, but I realized we weren't in a situation where any sort of romance would be appropriate. Our friends were out there, frightened or at the very least wondering if rescue would ever come. If I hadn't gone to talk with Rafe, I'd be with them.

It was wrong to feel any sense of happiness, and yet at the same time, I didn't want Bio-Chrome dictating my emotions.

I worked my way out of Rafe's embrace and swept my arm in an arc, indicating the cavern. "I was trying to straighten things up, but I guess it's pointless."

Rafe skimmed his thumb along my cheek, his light touch still enough to cause some discomfort from the swelling. I'd avoided looking for a mirror, not wanting to know how badly my eye had blackened from the fight last night. It was hard to believe that only a day had passed.

"Not pointless," Rafe said. "We'll have to pack it up eventually when we decide to move everything to another lair." He gave me an understanding smile. "Besides, we'll need to rest tonight before we start out after them."

We began working together to put things into containers and stack them against the wall.

I peered over at Rafe. He was focused on his task of stacking food items into a container. His dark hair framed his handsome face, and I could see determination written in every line of his features. Connor and Lucas weren't the only ones who were angry. Rafe usually kept all his emotions bottled up, as though he was afraid that if he let them out, he wouldn't be able to stuff them back inside. He'd released them briefly last night when he'd fought with Connor, and then he'd taken control of himself again.

But since the summer solstice he'd revealed so much to me: some of his vulnerabilities, some of his ambitions, some of the wildness that made him uniquely Rafe. If I had to make my choice at that exact moment, I wasn't entirely certain that I wouldn't choose him.

By the time we had things tolerably straightened, I was starting to feel claustrophobic. We each grabbed some protein bars and a couple of plastic bottles of juice and went outside. We climbed a short rise that gave us a spectacular view of the forest bathed in the light of a quarter moon.

"A little over a week to go," I said quietly, referring to how little time was left before the next full moon. "Do you think we'll have them back by then?"

Rafe wrapped his hand around mine where it rested in my lap. The gesture carried no sexual overtones; it was simply for reassurance. "I'm sure of it."

But even while we were trying to save our friends, I had some soul searching and decision making to take care of.

Any other time, what we were doing tonight, watching the stars together, would have seemed romantic. Instead we were simply waiting out the passage of time.

"Rafe?"

"Hmm?"

I took a deep breath. "Until we free the others, whatever you feel for me, want from me, whatever I've started to feel for you . . . we need to put it on hold. Our focus has to be on getting Kayla, Lucas, and Connor away from Bio-Chrome."

"Understood."

"Good."

He started to pull his hand away and I closed mine more firmly around it. "But we can still offer comfort, strength. We can be there for each other."

"Okay."

"I don't want to sleep alone." After what I'd seen happen that morning, I wasn't certain that I ever wanted to be alone again.

"You won't have to," he said quietly.

Just then, I saw a star shooting across the sky. I could think of so many things to wish for, but I chose the one that meant the most to me.

I wish . . . I hope we all come out of this alive.

Within the circle of Rafe's arms, I was able to sleep. When I opened my eyes, however, we weren't alone. Mason stood over us, larger than I remembered him. He was holding a silver gun, pointing it at me, and somehow I knew it contained silver bullets—one of the weapons to which we are vulnerable.

"I can't let you rescue them," he said in a soft, menacing voice.

He quickly shifted the gun over to Rafe and fired.

I screamed.

Arms came around me.

"Lindsey, wake up! You're dreaming. It's just a dream."

I opened my eyes for real this time. Rafe was holding me. Trembling, I collapsed against him. "Oh, God, it was horrible. Mason killed you."

"Bastard," he muttered through a slight grin.

I tightened my arms around him. "It's not funny."

"It was just a dream. I'm fine."

But still . . . the dream had seemed so real.

"What time is it?" I asked.

"Time for us to get going."

I nodded, but neither of us made an effort to get up. I wished so much that things were different, but wishing wasn't going to make it happen. I took a few more minutes to draw strength from Rafe's embrace. Then I began to prepare for whatever the day would bring.

While I gathered food for us, Rafe grabbed some hidden cans of gasoline and refueled his bike before rolling it outside. When I had stuffed as many supplies into my backpack as possible, I went out to meet him.

He was sitting on his bike, staring into the woods.

"We're going to ride?" I asked.

"No, too much noise. They'd hear us coming. But I want to teach you a few things in case you need to drive." He swung his leg back and got off the bike. Patting the seat, he said, "Sit here."

"You're not thinking I can drive that."

He sighed. "I think you need to know the basics just in case something happens to me and you need to get the hell out of Dodge."

My stomach tightened into a knot of fear. "Nothing is going to happen to you."

"I'm not planning on it, and both Connor and Lucas know how to drive it, but still . . ." He arched a dark brow and slapped his hand on the seat again.

Taking a deep breath, I set the backpack down. I straddled the seat, leaned forward, and grabbed the handles. Rafe got on behind me, his arms brushing up against my sides as he placed his larger hands over mine.

My breath hitched inappropriately with his nearness. At any other time, I thought I would have enjoyed the lesson, would have found his instruction incredibly sexy. But right now we were fighting for our lives and the lives of our friends.

"Okay, here's what you need to know," he said and his breath wafted along the side of my neck, causing a shiver of pleasure to cascade through me.

I tried to focus on his words and not on how wonderful it felt to have him so close to me. He explained the hand levers, the clutch, the brakes, the throttle, how to shift and brake using the foot controls. The concepts were easy, but the way everything had to be timed . . .

"I'll probably kill myself. Maybe I should just run," I said when he told me to take him back through the motions of starting the bike.

He chuckled low, a sound I was worried I'd never hear again. It warmed me, gave me hope that we would survive this.

I went through several mock sessions without actually turning on the bike. Rafe guided my hands and feet, giving me a sense of how to work the mechanics.

"Wish we could do a test run," Rafe said. "But I'm afraid they'll hear us."

"I think I've got it," I assured him.

He nodded. "Now, let's just hope you won't need the lesson after all."

We set off then, and because we knew the terrain well and were in great shape, both naturally and from all the hiking we do—unlike Mason's group, many of whom probably spent all their time sitting on stools, looking through microscopes—we were able to easily catch up with the group—even though Rafe was pushing the motorbike just in case, unable to shift, I needed to make a hasty escape. I also suspected that Kayla, Lucas, and Connor had done everything they could to slow the group down.

Rafe and I worked to stay upwind of them so their dogs wouldn't pick up our scent. While the group walked in a valley, we took the high ground instead, using rocks, boulders, trees, and brush to serve as cover as we kept them in our sights. When they stopped for lunch, so did we. Compared to the mercenaries, Mason appeared to be a hundred-pound weakling. I also noticed two of the lab techs—Ethan and Tyler—whom we'd met earlier in the summer.

"And to think I drank beer with that guy," Rafe said, pointing toward Ethan.

"They had us all fooled."

"Nah, I don't think Lucas ever trusted them—not completely."

"Are you sure we shouldn't try to rescue them tonight? Before they're someplace where we can't get to them easily?"

"Once darkness comes, I'll shift and prowl around. Maybe I can get close enough to Lucas to discuss tactics. I don't have any clear plans, and this is such a mess. I should have left you back at the lair."

"I wouldn't have stayed."

He gave me a wry grin. "Yeah, that's true."

He looked back toward Mason's group. They were on the move again.

And so were we.

We waited until nearly midnight to approach the camp, Rafe in wolf form and me—well, I was in the only form I could be at the moment. If we were spotted, Rafe would at least have the chance to get away. I probably wouldn't be as lucky. I knew Connor would be royally pissed if I was captured, but I wasn't going to hang back in the shadows as though I were useless.

More of the moon was visible tonight, and we were able to use its light to guide our way. Because my hair is such a pale shade of blond, I'd clipped it back and covered it with a dark bandanna so it wouldn't be visible. I'd even pulled a commando, smearing mud on my face so I would blend in better with the night and the forest. In truth, not yet being a full-fledged Shifter gave me an advantage: Because our fur tended to resemble the shade of our hair, I would be much harder to hide as a white wolf.

When we arrived at the edge of the camp, I felt an ache in my chest at the sight of my friends, sitting with their backs to a tree and their hands and feet bound. I thought if I could just get close enough, I could cut their bonds with the hunting knife I'd brought.

Rafe emitted a low, warning growl: *Don't even think about it.* I'd promised not to deviate from our plan, which was simply to observe.

I watched as Mason strolled toward our friends. He was good-looking, true, but in a Hollywood bad guy kind of way. Why hadn't I seen it before?

Mason knelt in front of Kayla and gripped her chin, forcing her to look at him. It also gave her a direct shot for spitting on him, and I wouldn't have been surprised if she had taken advantage of it.

"Look, I know Lucas is a werewolf," Mason said. "The wolf we caught had the same shade of fur as his hair—the exact same eyes. Human eyes. I know you broke him out of the cage."

"Do you realize how mental that sounds, Mason? That you believe people can really transform into animals? I admit to letting the wolf go, because they're a protected species in this park and you were abusing him. You didn't feed him or give him any water. You were killing him."

"We were weakening him so he'd be forced to shift. What about Connor? Is he one, too?"

"Mason, you're psychotic."

The crack of Mason's palm hitting her check echoed around us and was quickly followed by Lucas's low growl.

"Sure sounds like a wolf to me," Mason said.

I dug my fingers into my palms to remain focused, so I wouldn't do anything foolish. I wanted to yell at him to leave them alone, to let them go. I felt the animal inside of me tensing up, preparing to pounce. I was so angry that I thought I could take Mason down with nothing more than my human fists, fingernails, and teeth.

"How did you even know where to find us?" Kayla asked.

"Dallas. Misguided fool. He quit! *No one* quits Bio-Chrome. Our research is too important, and so is its secrecy. Took us a while to track him down in Tarrant. I figured there was only one reason he went there—to warn the werewolves. We'd been keeping a watch on the hotel, waiting for Dallas to return for his stuff. We were nearby listening when he arrived with that Rafe guy. We knew Lucas is a werewolf, so I assumed the other guys from our little hiking expedition are, too. The two of them talked about heading out on the motorcycle the next morning, so we put a tracking device on it. We figured Dallas was going to lead Rafe to the lab—it was our chance to catch one of the werewolves alone, and to stop Dallas's attempt at divulging the lab's location."

"So you *murdered* Dallas?"

"It wasn't intentional. When Dallas went into his room, we didn't expect him to come back out so soon. He caught a glimpse of Micah with his dog. He panicked and tried to run, but the dog attacked."

"His handler couldn't stop him?" I heard the anger in Kayla's voice. I didn't blame her. These guys thought anything was justified if it brought them closer to their goal of getting to us.

"Maybe we didn't do everything we could to stop it. So sue us," Mason said cruelly. "But in the end, Dallas was the enemy. He was willing to betray us. Good riddance, if you ask me."

He got up and walked away. I disliked his confident swagger, his whole attitude that because we were Shifters, we were less than human. It was driving me nuts; I had to do something.

I searched the ground until I found a small rock. Picking it up, I aimed carefully and threw it toward Connor to get his attention. His head came up and I could see him searching the forest. I crept out just a little from my hiding place behind a bush. His eyes widened and I read his lips when he mouthed a word he'd never use in front of his mother.

Go . . . *away!* he mouthed next.

I shook my head vehemently and mouthed back to him, *Be . . . ready.*

He shook his head. I sent him an air kiss, trying to offer him some reassurance that everything was going to be okay.

A hand came to rest lightly on my shoulder. I almost

screeched, before I realized it was Rafe. He nodded his head to the side. Hunched over, I followed him away from the camp until we reached a place where we intended to bed down for the night.

"I hate leaving them there," I told him.

"I know, but if you ever expose yourself like that again, I'm going to leave you behind. Do you know the risk you were taking?"

"I had no choice. I wanted to let them know that we were here, and that they need to be ready."

I could tell that he wasn't happy, but I also knew he couldn't argue my point.

In silence we ate some dry cereal that tasted like cardboard, although quite honestly I was so tense and worried that I didn't think I'd be able to appreciate even the tenderest steak.

"When this is over, I want to go to a fancy restaurant and eat the best meal of all time," I said.

"It's a date."

My heart did a little stutter, and my cheeks warmed. "Rafe—"

"I know we're not making any future plans, but you opened the door on that one. Besides, what would dinner hurt?"

It seemed ages ago that Connor and I had argued about Rafe, that Connor had suggested I go out with him. I nodded, pushing back my guilt. "I won't say no, but I won't promise yes."

"You know, I always thought it was supposed to be guys who had commitment problems," he teased.

As much as I appreciated the lighthearted banter, I kept silent. It just felt wrong when our friends were prisoners.

"Why don't you get some sleep?" he suggested.

"What about you?"

"We're so close to them that I want to keep watch." He leaned against a tree, and I stretched out on a sleeping bag beside him.

"Did you see the way Mason talks to them, the way he looks at them?"

"Like they're animals that have no rights?"

I nodded. "Yeah. Do you think all Statics view us as less than human?"

"I hope not. If this continues on, I just don't see how we can avoid the inevitable. We're going to be outed." He skimmed his fingers over my knuckles as though he needed some sort of contact. I knew I did, and I welcomed it.

"Do you have a plan for getting them away from Mason?" I asked.

"I'm working on it."

I released a small laugh. "In other words, no."

"We'll figure something out, Lindsey. Don't worry."

Only I *was* worried. It was really hard to try to figure out my feelings for Rafe and Connor with all this other, more important stuff bearing down on me. Their safety had to come first, and I couldn't be distracted by my emotions.

But they were there. They always seemed to be right there.

FIFTEEN

The following night, while I watched over Mason's encampment from a hidden place further up a mountain, Rafe shifted and went exploring. I brought my knees up to my chest, wrapped my arms around my legs, and wondered if it wouldn't be better to just try and rescue them now. Then we could all go searching for this stupid lab together.

The moon was way past its zenith when Rafe dropped down beside me. It always fascinated me how we could be as quiet in human form as in wolf form, as though stealth was inbred in us. I suppose it was, since part of us was predatory.

"I found it," he declared, smiling brightly.

Twisting around, I stared at him. "The lab?"

"Yeah. As slowly as they travel, it'll be another day or two before they reach it. I think it's time for a jail break."

I was almost giddy with the hope that this would all be over soon.

"You have a plan?" I asked.

"I think so. The problem is the dogs. I can shift, create a diversion, draw them—and hopefully some of the handlers—away. You can slip down, cut the ropes on Lucas, Kayla, and Connor. You and Connor can ride the bike out of here. I'll move it into place before I shift, so you can get to it easily enough. Kayla and Lucas can shift and run like the wind as soon as they're out of sight."

It sounded simple enough. Maybe too simple. We could have done this a couple of nights ago—though of course now we knew exactly where the lab was.

Two guards were patrolling the camp. Each had a dog with him.

"Okay, you're going to have to move quickly," Rafe said. "The dogs, along with their guards, should take off after me, but the dogs will probably make enough noise to wake everyone up. Hopefully it'll take them a while to get oriented."

I gave him a thumbs-up.

He made a move away from me, toward some bushes

where he would remove his clothes and shift. I grabbed his arm, stilling him. After everything that we'd been through, this moment seemed as though it should be bigger; after all, it was going to change everything, not only for us but for all Shifters. I held his brown gaze, a gaze that was at once warm and tender, but also determined and unafraid. It touched me deeply; it gave me courage.

"Be careful," I whispered.

"Always. And remember, you save yourself first."

I nodded, even though I wasn't certain it was a promise I was prepared to keep. How could he expect me to put myself before my friends? I mean, what kind of friend would that make me? Besides, I wasn't the one planning to serve myself up as bait for two Rottweilers with powerful jaws that could crush cement.

Rafe started to move away again, but his gaze dropped to my lips. "Ah, hell, I can only be so good."

He pulled me into his arms and kissed me. His lips were very much like his gaze: warm and tender, yet determined and oh-so-passionate. I couldn't help but wonder if, like me, he was fearful that we might never have another opportunity for this, so he wanted to make the most of it. He cradled my face between his hands, tilting my head slightly upward and deepening the kiss, until my toes, my fingers, my entire body simply wanted to curl into itself and savor every aspect of this moment.

All too quickly it was over, and he was dashing into the brush before I could plead with him to come up with another plan. I touched my fingers to my tingling lips.

A couple of minutes later, I saw the moonlight glinting off his fur as he slipped away to the far side of the camp, where one of the guards and a dog were headed. The other guard was on his way back to my end of the camp, where the prisoners were secured.

Suddenly, at precisely the same time, both dogs stilled and lifted their heads. Their ears flattened, and I heard their ominous growls. I knew a Rottweiler could move fast. I could only hope that Rafe could move even more quickly. They'd tear him up if they got their teeth into him.

All of a sudden both dogs took off running, barking, growling, pulling their handlers along with them. The guards finally released the leashes and just followed as best as they could. I darted out from my hiding place. Kayla saw me first, and her smile was so bright that it seemed as though she was simply welcoming me to a sleepover.

"Jesus, Lindsey, are you insane?" Connor asked, bringing me back to reality.

Ignoring his ungrateful greeting—and knowing it was

fear for me that prompted it—I was at the tree, sawing through the ropes that held Kayla before the guards were even beyond the camp.

"Hurry," Lucas said, and I heard in his voice how anxious he was to get into the thick of the battle.

"I'm trying."

As soon as I had Kayla free, I started on Lucas's bindings.

A light came on in the tent.

"I got Connor," Lucas said as soon as he was free. He took the knife from me. "Get out of here."

"Connor, meet me at Rafe's bike," I ordered before rushing toward where it was stashed. I knew I would be the slowest of all of us.

Kayla took my hand and we started running, our very lives depending on our speed.

"Hey! They're escaping!" I heard Mason shout. "Damn it! People! Get up, get after them!"

I didn't know if the guys would shift and take care of them or just use their fists, I had to trust that whatever they decided, they would succeed. Although I was the most vulnerable, I had a strong urge to turn back around, face them, and fight.

"Can you drive the bike if Connor doesn't get there?" Kayla asked, her breaths coming in short bursts.

"Yes, but I don't want to take off unless I know

everyone is safe. I don't think we'll get another chance at escape."

"I can't believe we got this one. You're awesome."

I heard the rapid pounding of footsteps. Glancing back, I saw that it was Connor and Lucas—so it seemed we Shifters weren't always quiet, not when our lives were in danger and we had to get away fast.

"The bike's over here," I shouted and headed for some brush.

"I'll take care of Lindsey," Connor said, coming up beside me to grab the bike and straddle it.

"Kayla and I are out of here," Lucas said, turning to go even as he spoke.

"Get on," Connor ordered as he turned the bike on and revved the throttle.

I straddled the seat and wrapped my arms around him. "What about Mason—"

"Left him and his buddies knocked out."

Knocked out. Not dead. I hoped that decision wouldn't come back to haunt us—although killing someone brought its own haunting effect.

With a roar of the engine, we took off, slicing through the forest. Suddenly there was a low growl, and one of the Rottweilers seemed to come out of nowhere. It leaped up and bit into my thigh. I screamed. Connor quickly veered, knocking the dog against a tree.

"You okay?" he asked, never reducing speed.

"Yes." But then I was aware of a distant explosion like gunfire. I felt a burning pain rip through my shoulder, and I clung more tightly to Connor.

I heard him curse and felt a sticky warmth seeping into my clothes.

"Hang on, Lindsey," I heard him yell, although the words seemed to come to me through water or some sort of barrier. "Stay awake! Stay alert!"

How did he know that I wanted to go to sleep? *Oh yeah, he can read my mind. No, he can't. Rafe can.*

"Stay with me, Lindsey!"

I wanted to. I really did. But my shoulder was on fire and my thigh ached. I wanted the agony to go away. Something seemed wrong about going to sleep, though— and then I realized that if I succumbed to the darkness hovering at the edge of my vision, I might tumble off the bike.

Yes, that's it. That's what would happen. I have to stay awake and hold on. If I let go of Connor, I'll have to add aching head to my list of pains.

"Talk to me, Lindsey. Tell me what you're feeling."

"My shoulder hurts."

"Mine, too. I think you were shot. The bullet went through."

Oh, that makes sense, I thought in a vague sort of

way. I was having difficulty holding onto my thoughts and analyzing the situation. But if I was shot, then that was the reason I could feel warmth turning cold on my back. But if the bullet went through me . . .

"Did the bullet hit you?" I asked, and was surprised to find that my words sounded somewhat slurred.

"Yes, but I can heal as soon as we stop."

"When will that be? I really want to sleep."

"I know, babe. Just hold on."

He'd never called me *babe* before. Never used any endearment for me. That was so sweet of him to do it now. I wanted to tell him that I'd been worried about him, but it was so difficult to form words. My mouth didn't want to work. I laid my head against his back. He was so comfortable.

"Lindsey?"

I heard him calling my name, but the darkness called more loudly, so I answered it.

"You were supposed to take care of her!"

"Well, if you'd kept the guards and their stupid dogs from turning back, she wouldn't have gotten hurt!"

The yelling and accusations continued. As I slowly broke through the fog of unconsciousness, I recognized the voices: Rafe and Connor. They were both alive, thank God, and clearly feeling way more energetic than I was.

"Guys, stop it!" Kayla demanded. "Don't make me

go all Dog Whisperer on your butts!"

I realized I was lying on the ground and she was sitting beside me. We were in one of our smaller lairs. So we'd gotten away. We were all safe. Weren't we?

"Lucas?" I rasped.

"You're awake," Kayla said, and squeezed my hand.

"Lucas?" I repeated.

"He's outside keeping guard. He spread some stuff around so the dogs would lose our scent. We think we're safe here. At least for a while. We need to get you home."

"How are you feeling?" Connor asked as he knelt beside me.

I could see Rafe standing a little off to the side, his worried gaze on me. Having two guys who wanted you was probably every girl's fantasy, but it came with so many complications—especially when you had to choose one. Soon.

"I'm hurt. Not too badly, though." The pain wasn't nearly as bad as I'd expected.

"We found a first-aid kit," Connor explained. "Had some pain meds in it. Your thigh is lacerated from where the dog pulled a Cujo on you, and your shoulder has a hole in it where the bullet went in and traveled out. We were able to pack your wounds to stop the bleeding, but Kayla is right. We need to get you home. We were thinking of tying you behind me on the bike."

I forced myself to grin. "That's not a ride we ever

went on at an amusement park."

"No." He brushed my hair off my brow. "We need to move quickly, before infection starts in."

I wrinkled my nose. "I'm going to scar." In a few more days, when I could shift, wounds would heal without scarring, but now—

"Maybe not. Or not too bad. And if you scar . . . well, I think scars are sexy."

I laughed lightly. "You do not."

"Sure, I do. Try to drink and eat a little. Then if you feel strong enough, we'll go."

I knew that even if I didn't feel strong enough, we needed to go. Because I wasn't going to get any better without medical attention.

Connor moved away. As much as I knew Rafe wanted to approach, he didn't. It wasn't his right. Until I made my decision, until I told Connor that I wasn't choosing him, he was my guy.

They both went outside. Maybe to check on the bike or on Lucas. Maybe to continue fighting where I couldn't hear them.

"They're both pretty worried about you," Kayla said as she twisted the top off a bottle of water before handing it to me.

I nodded, knowing she was trying to make a point: They were equal in their affections and concern for me.

Maybe she was also acknowledging that she understood the difficulty of my decision.

"Only a few nights until the full moon," she said quietly.

I groaned low. "I know."

"If you're still recovering, will your body delay its transformation?"

I slowly shook my head. "No such luck. The moon has some kind of mystic power over us. It's stronger than anything we face on earth. When it calls, we have to answer."

She handed me a peanut butter cracker. "You need protein," she said distractedly, then, "That is so weird— about the moon, I mean. I've felt it. I've gone through the transformation and it's like nothing I ever felt before. You can't prepare for it, and maybe that's the reason the guys don't talk about it. I know I tried to explain it, but it's as though for a short time your body isn't yours, but it *is* yours. It's foreign and yet it's so familiar. All because of a full moon."

"It's just the way it is," I said, using the bottled water to wash down the dry cracker. I guess it was easier for me to accept these things because I grew up with them.

"What if you choose the wrong guy?" she asked quietly.

"I don't know. I've known Connor forever. I've only

recently become aware of Rafe in that way. What if all this confusion and doubt is just because he's forbidden to me? How did you know with Lucas?"

"I just knew. Not much help, huh?"

"None at all."

Hearing footsteps, I glanced toward the entrance. Connor stood there. "Dawn's coming. We need to get going while you have the strength."

I nodded. "I'm ready."

He came over to help me stand. "You're gonna be all right, Lindsey."

I gave him a thumbs-up of assurance. Physically, maybe, I'd be fine. But my heart was still engaged in a battle, and I didn't know how it was going to end.

SIXTEEN

I kept opening and closing my eyes. And each time I opened them, there was a new scene before me.

Eyes open: The forest rushing past.

Eyes closed: Connor and me building a sandcastle.

Eyes open: Connor's back.

Eyes closed: Connor and me going skiing for the first time.

Eyes open: Rafe's worried face.

Eyes closed: Connor taking the blame when I broke my mother's favorite crystal vase.

Eyes open: Kayla making me drink water.

Eyes closed: Connor holding my hand when my grandmother died.

Eyes open: Lucas ordering me to fight.

Eyes closed: Connor giving me my first kiss.

Eyes open: Dr. Rayburn shining a light in my eyes.

Eyes closed: Connor and I making out in the back row at the movie theater.

Eyes open: Bright lights, a hard table, people staring down at me.

Eyes closed: Connor dancing with me at the prom.

Eyes open: My mother crying and combing her fingers through my hair.

Eyes closed: Connor declaring me as his mate.

Eyes open: My father, my strong dad, with tears in his eyes.

Eyes closed: Connor and me beneath a full moon.

Eyes open: Connor lying on a bed beside mine.

This time my eyes stayed open. I squinted at him, vaguely remembering the bullet hitting me. "Are you real?"

He smiled at me. "Yeah."

"Where are we?" My voice sounded as though it was coming from another room or another dimension, as though it wasn't even here with me.

"Wolford. The medical hallway."

I scrunched up my face. "This is no fun. You should just shift and heal."

"I did." He held up his arm and I could see a needle

with some kind of tubing coming out of it. "This is for you. You lost too much blood."

"You're giving me blood?"

"Yeah, we're the same type."

I thought I said *thank you* before drifting off into the peaceful realm of oblivion. I heard Connor say, "You're welcome."

The next time I woke up, my mom was sitting beside the bed. She poked a straw into my mouth and ordered me to sip. It was the best water I'd ever tasted.

"I'm tired," I mumbled, wondering how I could be tired when it seemed I'd been sleeping all the time.

"You've been through quite an ordeal. You should feel like getting out of bed in another day or so." With her fingers, she combed my hair back. "Connor saved your life, you know."

I furrowed my brow. "Really? I thought maybe it was the doctor."

"Connor wouldn't let the others stop on the journey back here. He gave you his blood. He checks on you several times a day."

"Are you a lobbyist?" I asked.

She gave an impatient huff. I closed my eyes and went back to sleep.

Mom was right. My strength was returning. By late afternoon the following day, I was ready for adventure.

"I'm really feeling strong enough to get out of bed now," I told my mom. I kept pushing the covers down. She kept lifting them back up to my chin. It was irritating to have her hovering around me.

"I think another day in bed is what you need."

"Mom." I rolled my eyes. "I really need to get out of here before I go crazy."

"This close to your full moon, your body is probably more resilient. I suppose if you took it very easy, didn't try anything too strenuous, it would be all right."

"Fine. I'll just sit around, but I need to do it out of this room." I shoved the blanket down; she brought it back up.

"I want to talk with you first about your . . . trans-formation."

We'd never had the transformation talk . . . or the sex one either.

"Mom, you're a little late. I've already talked with Kayla. She told me everything. I'm not afraid."

"You should be," she said sternly, taking me by surprise. Her face softened and she brushed my hair back from my brow. "You know that your father and I think the world of Connor."

"I know."

"And I know you've been hanging around with this Rafe boy. Now is not the time to get rebellious, Lindsey.

A bond develops during the transformation. Love deepens. A pact is sealed. A pact until death."

"I know that, Mom. Why do you think I'm so scared that I might be making a mistake with Connor?"

"You're not making a mistake with Connor. Rafe would be the mistake."

"How can you be sure?"

"Because I know you. And I know both of these boys. Connor is right for you."

In other words, they'd never accept Rafe. Brittany was so right. Our traditions bordered on the archaic.

"Thanks for the advice, Mom." This time when I shoved the covers down, she didn't pull them back up.

"I just want you to be happy," she said.

I scrambled out of bed and started limping to the bathroom, my thigh still sore.

"I just want to be happy, too."

Inside the bathroom, I removed the bandages and studied my wounds. They were healing nicely. The doctor had done a good job of closing them with tiny stitches, so I wouldn't have a horrible scar after all. If they weren't completely healed, the transformation should take care of them.

I washed up, combed out my hair, and put on a light layer of makeup. I slipped into shorts and a strapless top so nothing would rub against the wounds. I thought they needed fresh air as much as I did. Then I went in search of the others.

I found them all in the library, standing around a desk, studying a large map of the national forest. Even Brittany was there. But my attention was drawn to Connor and Rafe. Connor of the light hair, Rafe of the dark. Connor of the abundant grins, Rafe of the rare ones. Connor, the steady constant in my life. Rafe, the new and exciting element.

"Hey, you're alive," Brittany suddenly shouted, with genuine enthusiasm.

"Thanks to these guys," I said self-consciously as I moved toward the desk.

"I can't believe you all went after Bio-Chrome while I was dealing with campers."

"We didn't exactly go after them. We just followed them, trying to figure out where they had their lab. You probably had way more fun with Daniel."

She shook her head. "He's not a loser or anything, but I'm *so* not into being set up."

"But Brittany—"

"I'm going to be fine."

Okay, so she didn't want to talk about it. I guessed there were more important items on the menu of topics.

"So are you guys talking about how to get rid of that lab?" I asked.

"That's what we're trying to decide," Lucas said.

"Don't suppose you'd wait until after the next full moon . . . ," I suggested.

Connor leaned against the desk. "Actually we were just saying that there's no reason to rush. They're not going to tell the world we exist, because they want to keep us secret as long as possible."

"Want to keep their work secret," Kayla added.

"So what's the plan?" I asked.

Lucas sighed. "Not sure yet. Although they're not on actual national forest land, they are still surrounded by forest. Burning the place to the ground won't work, because it might ignite the forest as well."

"So we have to find a way to destroy it without destroying our home as well."

"Exactly."

"I'm going to talk with the elders. Whatever we decide, doing it during the next dark of the moon would probably be best."

"Under the cover of darkness makes it all sound kinda *Mission Impossible*-ish," Connor said.

"It will be," Lucas confirmed. "We'll want careful planning, not just to destroy the building, but to make a statement so Bio-Chrome will leave us in peace."

"Do you think they realize *all* the sherpas are Shifters?" Rafe asked. "Do you think everyone is in danger?"

I shifted my attention over to him, and he held my

gaze. I read a challenge there: *Make your choice*. The truth was, I already had.

"I don't think they've figured that out," Lucas said. "I don't think they know how widespread we are. Besides, they still have no proof. They've never actually seen any of us shift. If they find our clothes, so what? Maybe they're a little more convinced that whatever my brother told Mason about Shifters is true. But they're scientists. They deal with facts."

"How are you going to discourage them from coming after us again?" Kayla asked.

Lucas shook his head. "I haven't a clue. But we'll figure something out. We have time."

He ended the meeting. He and Kayla left to go talk with the elders. Brittany left, too, as did Rafe, though reluctantly.

"Do you really think we can convince them to leave us alone?" I asked Connor.

"Probably not, but we can try." He moved around the desk and took my hand. "You feeling okay?"

Physically or emotionally? I thought.

"Just a little tired." I decided to go with the physical answer. It was so much easier to deal with.

"You feel up to a walk?"

I didn't. My energy level was quickly declining, but I nodded. I had to explain some things to Connor. He was my best friend, besides Kayla. He was the friend I'd had the longest.

We made our way outside and walked to where trees grew in earnest. Although a wrought-iron fence surrounded Wolford, the property was large enough that we could go into the woods while still protected by the fence—or as protected as we could be when considering that bullets still could zip through. I'd always considered myself invincible, but now I knew that death could come quickly and unexpectedly.

"I've got a birthday present for you," Connor said quietly, "but it'll have to wait until after your transformation."

My birthday had come while I was recovering. I didn't even remember it. "You don't have to give me anything," I said.

"I know I don't *have* to, but I want to."

He stopped walking, reached into his jeans pocket, and brought out a small velvet box. My heart galloped.

"Oh, Connor."

"Open it."

With shaking hands, I did. Inside was a gold chain with a small, perfectly round pearl dangling from it. "It's beautiful."

"It's supposed to represent the full moon," he said.

I looked up at him. "It's perfect. Thank you."

"I knew you'd like it."

He knew so much about me. I couldn't believe how his gift overwhelmed me. Maybe because I'd almost died, everything seemed so much more important. When he took my hand, my fingers closed around his.

We took several steps in silence. Once we could have spent hours together without talking, and it had seemed the most natural thing in the world. Now it just seemed as though a lot of unsaid thoughts hung heavily between us.

I shoved them to the back of my mind and concentrated on the healing properties of the forest. I was already beginning to feel my strength returning, which was good, because when the full moon arrived, I'd be facing an ordeal that would require all the energy I could muster. But before that, I needed a question answered.

"Do you ever wonder if you declared me too soon?" I asked.

Connor tilted his head as though looking at me from a different angle might help him decipher my strange mood. "No. I've always known you were the one. I love you, Lindsey. I always have."

There it was. The words he could say so easily. Something Rafe had never said. Quite honestly, I couldn't see Rafe uttering those words—but that didn't mean he didn't feel them. It just meant that he isn't as free about revealing his emotions as Connor is.

Connor held my gaze, and I could see how much my doubts had hurt him. Yet he never gave up on me; he always put me first.

"Your moon is almost here, Lindsey. You have to make a choice."

I shook my head. "No, I don't have to *make* it. I already made it." I took a deep breath. "It's you, Connor. I love you."

He looked stunned. "What about Rafe? What about your doubts?"

I shook my head. "It's you. And my doubts are gone. This is going to sound strange, but I think getting shot might have been the best thing that could have happened to me. It gave me a chance to just reflect. I saw the kaleidoscope of my life and no matter how I turned it, I saw you."

A wide grin spread across his face. "You're serious?"

I smiled. "I'm serious."

He pulled me into his arms and kissed me with excitement and enthusiasm. When we finally came up for air, I was dizzy.

"I was thinking we'd go to the waterfall lair for your transformation," he said.

The first transformation always occurred in the forest, away from other Shifters. A guy went through it alone. He just went off—and when he came back, he was changed. The girl always went off to a secluded place with her mate. The area around the waterfall was one of the most beautiful in the forest. Our lair was hidden behind the waterfall. It was a favorite place for many a couple. My father had taken my mother there. It provided a little extra romance for the occasion.

"Sounds amazing."

"If we're going to go to the waterfall, we should leave in the morning. If you feel strong enough," he added.

I nodded. "I will." Suddenly I felt so weary. "But right now, I need to lie down."

He took my hand and we started walking back toward the mansion. Why did I feel as though I was being watched?

I glanced slyly off to the side. And there was the beautiful black wolf, watching.

When I woke up from my nap, Brittany was sitting on the window seat, gazing out as twilight fell. I'd gone to the room that I usually shared with her and Kayla. I was feeling strong enough that I didn't need to be nursed anymore—and getting away from my mom for a while was a nice bonus.

With a yawn, I sat up and pushed the pillows behind my back. "So where are you going for your transformation?"

"Not the waterfall." She didn't turn toward me.

"Brittany, who's going with you?"

She didn't answer. She just sat there. I climbed out of bed, walked over to the window, and sat on the thick pillow. "You can't go through this alone."

"That's just an old wives' tale."

"What if it's not?"

She looked at me, something hard in her blue eyes. "Then it's a seriously messed-up evolutionary tactic. I mean, really, it's totally sexist. If guys can go through it alone, we can, too."

"You could ask . . . Rafe."

Her eyes softened with sadness. "So you chose Connor?"

"He's always been there for me."

"Is that a good enough reason, though? Do you love him?"

"Yes, I love him."

"But do you love him enough?"

"God, Brittany. What is with you? Do you love him? Is that what this is all about?" I'd asked her before but she'd never given me a definite answer.

She looked out the window again. "Doesn't matter. You're the only one he's interested in. I'll just be the lone she-wolf. I'll become legendary. Maybe I'll start a new trend, and we'll do away with all this destined mate nonsense."

"Do you really think that it's nonsense?"

"I think we're locked in the old ways. I think we need to come into the twenty-first century." She slid her gaze over to me. "You could always go through it alone, too. Choose your mate later."

I shook my head. "I've already chosen my mate."

She got up. "We should probably go down for supper."

I looked out the window and saw Rafe standing at the edge of the woods. "I'll be down in a little bit."

I waited until I knew she would be almost to the dining hall before I slipped out of the room and headed down the back stairs that led outside. I hurried across the grass to the woods, which were quickly becoming lost in shadows as the sun descended and the growing moon began to rise.

I slipped between the trees. "Rafe?"

In his usual quiet way, he was suddenly in front of me. I leaned back against a tree.

Rafe put his arm over my head, pressing his forearm against the tree. He trailed his finger along my cheek. "So you knew I was out here. That means you came to see me."

Nodding, I gazed into his beautiful dark-brown eyes. I didn't want to do this, didn't want to hurt him, but he deserved to hear it from me. "Connor and I are going to leave for the waterfall tomorrow." *Oh, this is hard.* "I just wanted you to know . . . I'm going with him."

"So you've chosen him," he said with deadly calm. The words were a statement, not a question.

"It was always supposed to be him," I said.

"Why? Because that's what your parents want?"

"No, because it's what I want," I stated clearly, irritated that everyone seemed to think my parents were responsible for my choices. "He's a good guy."

"Yeah." He gave a harsh laugh. "Makes this hard."

"I guess you'd challenge and kill him otherwise, right?"

"If he was a jerk—in a heartbeat."

My own heart sped up. "Well, don't," I ordered sternly. "I don't want him hurt. And if you're looking for a mate, Brittany is available."

"I don't feel for Brittany what I feel for you. Don't you get that?"

"Rafe, maybe if we'd noticed each other sooner—"

Another burst of harsh laughter came from him. "I've noticed you since middle school, but you were always hanging out with Connor. You never gave anyone else a chance."

Until this summer I hadn't even considered anyone else, hadn't wanted anyone else. What was wrong with me? It had always been Connor.

"You told me that you didn't notice me until this summer," I reminded him.

"The strong feelings I have for you didn't hit me until this summer, but I've always noticed you. When the full moon comes, and you're with Connor, think about what you could have had," he said.

Then he kissed me deeply and thoroughly. I knew I should have protested, should have pushed him away. Instead I wrapped my arms around his shoulders, knowing this would be the last kiss we'd ever share. I wanted it to last forever, even though I knew it couldn't.

When he drew back, I felt what I always did with Rafe: confused. *Maybe I should do what Brittany suggested,* I thought. *Just go through the transformation by myself and decide later who should be my mate.* But then I remembered what Kayla had said about how wonderful it was to go through it with someone you cared for, someone you loved.

"Good-bye, Rafe," I said quietly and walked away from him.

He didn't try to stop me. And I thought that probably said it all.

Because I knew deep down that Connor would have tried to stop me from walking away.

SEVENTEEN

"Your dad and I will be here when you get back," my mom said as she hugged me tightly. "You won't regret your decision," she whispered near my ear.

I really could have gone my entire life without that comment. It started to raise those stupid doubts again that Connor was her choice and not mine.

Dad embraced me. "My little girl." Then he shook Connor's hand, and Mom hugged Connor.

When Connor and I were finally walking through the woods, I said, "Glad that's over."

"They're just worried about you. How are your wounds?"

"Not bad." I was limping a little and my shoulder

ached, but I'd heal during the transformation. I was feeling much stronger, but neither Connor nor I were pushing ourselves to our hiking limits.

We were traveling quietly, remaining alert. Every now and then, he would hand his backpack and clothes to me, shift while I closed my eyes, and search a wide circle around us. Although his senses were heightened as a human, as a wolf they were even more so.

That night, we took turns keeping watch. The second night a deer approached our camp—it was the only stranger we encountered.

In the afternoon, we arrived at our destination. We climbed the escarpment and followed a winding trail into the small valley that was enclosed by two mountains. On one side of the clearing was the waterfall. On the other was a forest that swept back and up to the other mountain. This was a well-hidden place, not easily found unless someone knew the way. We weren't concerned that Mason and his group would find us. They had no reason to look for us here.

And in just a few hours, after the full moon rose in the night sky, I'd have the ability to shift and escape just as quickly as Connor could.

Connor took my hand and led me around the pond to where the waterfall emptied with a mighty rush of cascading water. It was noisy here, and as we grew nearer the water's power created a gust that blew my braids around my shoulders. We slipped behind the waterfall into a cavern.

This was my favorite of all the lairs. Food and essentials were stacked in crates. Connor turned on a battery-powered light. Shrugging out of my backpack, I walked around finding comfort here. It seemed there were a thousand things that Connor and I should say to each other, but we'd barely talked at all as we traveled.

I thought about Brittany and wondered where she'd gone to experience her first transformation. I wondered if she was afraid to be alone. I didn't think I'd be scared, exactly, but I'd definitely be nervous.

"What are you thinking?" Connor asked.

"About Brittany. She's going to go through this alone." I glanced around. "Do you think she'll be okay? Should she have come with us? Could you have helped her, too?"

"I don't think we can bond with two people."

My stomach knotted up. I knew I was supposed to be concentrating on my own transformation, my own needs, but something about Brittany was bothering me. I was really worried about her. I wondered if Rafe might be with her, then selfishly wished he wouldn't. *If he can't be mine,* I thought, *I don't want him to bond with anyone.* And that made me a cold bitch. What if I'd made a mistake choosing Connor? I didn't believe I had, but suddenly there was this niggling concern . . . probably just nerves as the moon's arrival approached.

"Here's everything that we'll need," Connor said, removing a large crate from the stack. He opened it.

As I walked over, he removed a black robe and then handed me a beautiful silvery-white robe. It looked like something fairy queens always wore in the movies.

"Makes it easier for us to shift. We're not encumbered with clothes," he said.

"I'd heard about that," I said, taking the robe. It was soft and silky; how nice it would feel against my skin.

"We have a few hours yet. What do you want to do?" he asked.

"I'm really tired. Could I take a nap?"

"We probably both should. Tonight will be . . . draining."

I watched as he arranged sleeping bags and quilts to create a soft place for us to sleep. We were only going to sleep, and yet I felt nervous about it. My skin suddenly felt incredibly sensitive, as though I could actually feel dust motes landing on it. I knew it was probably my body preparing for the upcoming transformation, but it was a strange sensation, and I imagined Connor holding me, his hands skimming over my back or along my face. I thought I'd be able to feel every groove of his fingertips.

"What do you like best about being in your wolf form?" I blurted, wondering why I was suddenly so skittish. This was Connor. My mate. My destiny. Hadn't we been together forever?

He stopped what he was doing. Still crouching, he rested his forearms on his knees and looked up at me. "I like the way everything seems more alive. Sounds are sharper; colors are brighter. I can hear my own heart thundering. It's a trip—probably like tripping, in a way. Not that I'd know."

"You've never done drugs?"

"No. Why would I? Why would any of us when we can shift? That's an indescribable rush of its own."

"Do you ever lose sight of who you are?"

"No. You still think human thoughts; they just tend to have a slightly savage edge to them. In human form, if I were attacked, I'd think about beating the guy up. In wolf form, I'd probably think about killing him. It's all about survival when we're in animal form."

I crossed my arms over my chest, feeling self-conscious about the thought of sleeping in Connor's arms, which was silly because I'd slept in his arms before. "I never talked about this with my parents."

"Me, either." He patted the quilts. "Come on. You look like you're about to drop dead."

I stretched out on the padding and he lay down beside

me, letting me use his shoulder as a pillow.

"I feel like I want to crawl out of my skin," I told him.

"It's just your body preparing for the transformation."

"Does it feel this . . . sensitive all the time?"

"Yeah, but you get used to it."

I couldn't imagine, but I trusted Connor.

"Will you wake me at sunset?" I asked. "I want some time to prepare."

"Yeah."

My eyelids grew heavy and my muscles began to relax into that never-want-to-move-again phase that comes just before sleep. Drowsily, I asked, "Connor, should I be afraid?"

His arms tightened around me. "No, Lindsey."

I drifted off to sleep and dreamed that when I awoke, I was a beautiful wolf.

Connor kept his promise and woke me shortly after the sun had set. The next time it rose, I would be changed. Anticipation thrummed through me as I ate the simple meal of rations that were supposedly also served on space shuttles. We packed our lairs as though we were survivalists, including food items with far-off expiration dates. Who knew when we'd need them or how long we'd have to hide out?

Connor had set a flashlight between us, its light

pointing upward, and draped a gauzy blue scarf over it. I didn't know where he got the scarf but it muted the light, giving it a little bit of a romantic glow.

"I know blue is your favorite color," he said.

It was. He knew everything about me.

"Maybe we'll go out to a fancy restaurant later this week, to finally celebrate your birthday," he said.

I thought back to Rafe offering to take me out to dinner, but then I pushed the memory back down where it belonged.

"Remember when our moms made us take those etiquette lessons?"

He grinned. "Yeah."

I'd been twelve at the time; he'd been fourteen. They'd thought we needed to know which forks to eat with if we went to a fancy dinner at someone's house.

"And you kept burping," I reminded him.

"Hey! It wasn't just me. You were the one who suggested we burp 'Somewhere Over the Rainbow.'"

I laughed, remembering how we'd both gotten into trouble for not taking the lesson seriously.

"I mean, really, why does a formal dinner need so much silverware?" I asked.

"Beats me. I'm pretty much living on pizza at college, so what does it matter?"

"I miss you when you're at school," I said.

"I miss you, too. One more year."

"I might graduate early, maybe December."

"Really? That'd be great."

I nodded. "Yeah, it would be." And I was just babbling about nothing now, trying to get my stomach to relax.

Connor picked up our trash. "I'm going outside. Just meet me there when you're ready."

I watched as he grabbed the black robe. When he was gone, I sat with my legs crossed and did some deep breathing exercises. I flexed my muscles, did some stretching, and listened as my joints popped. Then I rose to my feet and began to prepare myself.

I fought not to think about Rafe, to wonder what he might be doing tonight.

Connor was my destiny.

I unbraided my hair and brushed it until it shone to a white gloss, like taffy I'd once seen beaten to a shine. I left it loose and fought not to think about Rafe asking me to do just that. I smoothed some shimmery body lotion over my arms and legs, thinking it would both settle me in my human skin and help my body stretch.

I looked at my reflection in the mirror. All I wore was a white velvet robe. In some ways I looked older; in some ways I looked the same. The same would be true of me when I shifted.

I turned from the mirror and walked to the entrance of the cavern, slipped out from beneath the curtain of water, and circled the still pool that would soon reflect the rising moon.

Connor stood there, waiting for me, his dark-blond hair brushed back, his sapphire-blue eyes calm. He wore a black robe. He held out his hand to me, and I placed my palm against his. His fingers, so sure and steady, closed around mine.

"Nervous, Lindsey?" he asked.

"Yeah, a little." I released a self-conscious puff of breath. "I've been waiting for this moment my whole life."

"Me, too."

"But you've already transformed."

"Not with you."

Leaning in, he brushed his lips over mine. My heart stuttered, and I fought not to think about Rafe. *Connor is my friend. I care about him. . . .*

"We should go," I said, before my thoughts traveled down a path that would lead to disaster.

Holding my hand, he led me to the middle of the clearing. I could see the full moon: so large, so bright, so yellow. My transformation wouldn't begin until it reached its zenith.

Connor and I faced each other, waiting for the moment. I took a deep breath, trying to calm my racing heart.

Then I heard the growl—low, deep, and challenging.

Connor and I both turned our attention to the forest.

Near the trees, a lone black wolf snarled. I would have recognized those chocolate-brown eyes anywhere.

"Don't do this, Rafe," Connor commanded sternly.

The wolf crouched and bared his teeth. A dare. A challenge.

Connor looked back at me. "Which one of us do you want to win?"

He hesitated only a heartbeat before he threw off his robe and ran toward the wolf. Then Connor leaped up and, in the blink of an eye, transformed into a golden wolf. The black wolf lunged at him. They collided in midair: light and dark.

I watched in horror, knowing what Connor had really asked me: *Which one of us do you want to die?*

We are human, but we are also beast, and in our world a challenge isn't made lightly. A challenge is a fight to the death.

I knelt in the grass and felt the tears washing down my face. I hadn't been able to give Connor an answer. The battle that had been raging in my heart all summer had transcended into one of flesh and blood.

Tonight, beneath a full moon, someone I loved would die.

EIGHTEEN

They clashed, they snarled, they bared their teeth. They weren't kidding here. They were both alpha males trying to claim their mate. At that moment I hated what we were, hated that we could be reduced to wild animals governed by instinct instead of by our hearts and minds.

"Don't do this!" I yelled, but they ignored me.

This was worse than the fight they'd had in the cave. I'd sustain more than a black eye if I tried to get between them. I was likely to end up with a gaping hole in my throat.

They broke apart and then came back together,

growling and snapping their jaws. Shifters are larger and stronger than the wolves in the wild. Connor and Rafe were well matched, and they weren't afraid to fight, to tear at each other.

I pushed myself to my feet. I had to stop this madness. I'd loved Connor forever and loved Rafe just a short time. Which was more important: the length of time or the intensity of emotion?

They separated, and the golden wolf slowly circled the black wolf. Rafe seemed to be hurt. When we are bitten by one of our kind, the wound we receive doesn't heal as quickly as those delivered by other animals. Something in our saliva stops the healing process that usually occurs when we're injured while in wolf form. I wondered what Mason might do with that information. If you had no vulnerabilities, you could never be destroyed. We, however, could be destroyed.

Judging by how heavily Rafe was breathing, how still he was, how he was sizing up Connor and waiting . . . I knew he'd been hurt. In the moonlight, I could see a dark dampness on his fur. It flowed from near his throat, the most vulnerable part of his wolf form. If Connor had nicked Rafe's carotid artery, though, he'd have bled out already. That hadn't happened, but it looked like he'd gotten him good anyway.

I knew Connor, had seen him fight, knew he could be

lethal. I knew he had the habit of sizing up his opponent and determining his weakness—and then he'd strike. He suddenly became still, put his weight back on his haunches, and I knew he was going to go for the kill. . . .

I also knew that Connor's primal instincts had taken over. He always worked so hard to control them, to be more human than beast, to be civilized. When Connor emerged from his barbaric haze, if Rafe was dead, Connor would never forgive himself. I suspected that if Rafe came out the victor, he would live with regrets over killing Connor. I also knew that regardless of who died, I would always blame myself because I hadn't been strong enough to make my choice before it was too late.

"No!" I screamed as I ran for them.

The moonlight washed over me and pain shot through my body. It was more intense than I had ever expected. I doubled over and fell to my knees.

Connor launched himself at Rafe.

Rafe lunged for him in return. I heard the clash of bone and flesh. I struggled to my feet and staggered toward them. I felt as though my bones had turned into shards of glass.

I had to do this. I had to reach them. Since the beginning of summer I'd begun to have doubts. I'd shared my doubts with them and made them each feel less than who they were. This wasn't their battle to fight. It was mine.

I thought about the joy I felt when I was with Rafe. I thought about how I always wanted him to touch me, how desperately I wanted to touch him. I remembered how he'd admitted hungering for me. That desire for him lived inside me, too, terrifying me with its intensity. I'd been afraid to give in to it, to embrace it. I'd feared that it was temporary.

But I knew now that it was the call of my mate, the lure of my destiny. If I didn't accept and fight for it now, I would lose it forever.

Rafe and Connor were rolling over the ground, snarling and snapping at each other. Two feral beasts, exhibiting nature at its most untamed—but inside there was still that spark of human that separated us from the true wolves. I was counting on that now.

I dropped to my knees and cried, "I choose Rafe! With all that I am and all that I will be, I choose Rafe as my mate."

They both stilled at once. I looked into the brown eyes of the one who, in only a short time, I'd come to love more than anything. In those brown depths, I didn't see victory or satisfaction. I saw instead a love so deep, so powerful, that if I hadn't already been on my knees I would have fallen to them.

I shifted my gaze to the eyes of blue. I saw hurt pride

there—but no deep loss, no true devastation.

"I'm sorry, Connor," I said softly. Pain ripped through me and I bit back a scream. "I wanted it to be you. You've been with me for every important moment in my life— but this moment belongs to Rafe. I love him so much that it scares me. You were the easier choice, but the wrong one."

The black wolf pulled away from the blond one and moved beyond my vision. The blond wolf slowly rolled over to his feet. With a last look in my direction, he loped off into the forest.

Agony poured through me like molten fire. I doubled over, refusing to scream.

Suddenly, Rafe was kneeling beside me, the robe wrapped around him, his hands grasping my arms. "Lindsey, do you accept me as your mate?"

I looked into his beautiful chocolate eyes, could see the blood flowing from his shoulder where Connor had dug his fangs into Rafe's flesh. I nodded. "Yes, Rafe. I love you."

He pulled me close, held me tightly, and kissed me. I concentrated on the strength in his arms, the power of his kiss. It was what I needed to distract me. The pain began to recede, like waves that had washed up on the shore. It had seemed so powerful, so overwhelming, but now it was easing away and all that surrounded me was

Rafe—Rafe and whatever he might feel for me.

He'd fought for me. It was something the ancients had done, but as far as I knew no one had done it in modern times. I was overwhelmed that he would risk so much for me, overwhelmed that Connor had answered the call to fight—and then walked away. I didn't have time to think about that or what it might mean.

All I could think about was Rafe and all the strange sensations running through me, as though my blood now contained a thousand glittering stars. Rafe deepened the kiss. I was tingling all over with a sensation that seemed caught between pleasure and pain, and then I felt as though I'd been harboring fireworks that suddenly burst through me. . . .

Rafe was no longer kissing me, but was nuzzling his cold nose against mine. He was a wolf.

And so was I.

I glanced down. I was just as I'd always thought I'd be. A beautiful white, like the Arctic wolf.

You're so pretty.

The words popped into my head, and I realized they weren't my thoughts. They were Rafe's.

I can hear your thoughts.

If wolves could grin, he was grinning.

Forgive me for challenging Connor, but I couldn't give you up that easily, not without a fight.

You could have been killed.

I'm not usually one for corny thoughts, but if I couldn't be your mate, I didn't care what happened.

Don't ever do that again.

I won't.

I glanced around. *Where's Connor? He'll always be my friend. I should go to him.*

Trust me. He'll want to be alone for now. You can find him later. He nuzzled my throat. *I want to show you the world through the eyes of a wolf.*

He started to lope away, and I rushed after him. It was strange that my heart no longer had any doubts. It seemed silly now that I hadn't known my own heart's desire.

Rafe was the one. The one I loved deeply, the one I wanted with me through all the challenges in my life. I knew that now, could feel it just as I felt my own heart pumping throughout my wolf's body.

We climbed to a spot on the mountain where we could look out over the national forest and up into the vast expanse of sky. In the shape of a wolf, I felt a stronger connection to it all, as though I were more attuned to nature.

Part of me was sad that Connor wasn't here with me. He'd been with me through so many important moments—but now I understood that I was never meant to share this moment with Connor. It was Rafe's moment. It had always been his.

I looked over at Rafe. *I love you.*

In the silence of the night, I heard his answer.

I love you, too.

NINETEEN

I can't explain what it's like to take another form. On the one hand, everything is totally different: the way I move, the way I think, the way I perceive the world. On the other hand, none of it is strange. It's still me.

After what must have been hours but seemed like only minutes, Rafe and I returned to the clearing. I closed my eyes and imagined myself as I'd always been—even though I'd never again be what I was before the wonder of this transformation. But I saw myself as a girl. I felt a tingling, like an electrical current, running through me—and when I opened my eyes, I was once again in human form. Reaching down, I picked up the robe I'd been wearing before the change and draped it over my shoulders.

Looking around, I saw Rafe coming out of the forest. Wearing his jeans, he held his shirt in one hand and his shoes in the other.

Suddenly I felt more exhausted than I'd thought possible. I swayed. Immediately he was beside me, wrapping his arm around me, drawing me up against his side. I felt a soul-deep connection with him that I'd never experienced with Connor. Part of me was sad, hoping that my childhood friend would be okay. A part of me even missed him. But most of me was still just blown away by all that had happened on this night. I finally knew who my true mate was. I rested my head in the curve of his shoulder.

"It can wear you out the first time," Rafe said quietly, pressing a kiss against my temple.

"Only the first time?"

"It gets easier."

With my first transformation, I had finished healing. The gash on my leg and the hole in my shoulder were both gone, having left behind only minimal scars. The wounds Rafe had received tonight, the result of a Shifter bite, were slower to heal but weren't life threatening; they'd leave scars, but then, I had a couple as well. And I have to admit it: I thought his scars were sexy because they were a testament to what he had been willing to give up for me.

He led me toward the cavern behind the waterfall. Once inside, he released his hold on me, tossed his shirt and shoes to the side, and began preparing a place for us to sleep. I sank down onto the ground and drew my legs up beneath me. I watched as he worked, arranging only one pallet. Tonight there was no question that we would sleep together. For the first time it would be without guilt, without feeling as though I were betraying Connor.

I'd made my choice—and by leaving, he'd accepted it.

I thought about putting on my clothes, but my skin was still incredibly sensitive. I remembered how my mother always wore silk; perhaps this increased sensitivity was a side effect.

I shoved myself to my feet. "Let me help."

Crouching beside the mound of blankets and pillows, he looked up at me. I thought I'd never grow tired of gazing into his warm, brown eyes, seeing the tenderness there that he felt for me. "No. This is part of the ritual."

Suddenly I was a little nervous. Girls always talked about the transformation and being with their mates, but they never really talked about what came after. I knelt opposite him. "Really?"

"Yeah. Back in the old days this would be the first night that a couple would sleep together."

"How do you know that?"

"Mating 101."

I laughed, and some of the tension eased.

"Hey, I'm not kidding," he said, his voice serious, his smile warm. "The elders make us sit through a lecture on how we're supposed to treat our mates."

I dropped my head back and groaned. "Brittany is so right. We're totally archaic."

My stomach tightened as I thought about her. I shifted my attention to the waterfall.

"She'll be all right," Rafe said.

I wasn't so sure. "If I'd made the right choice earlier, Connor might have been with her." Had my indecision killed her?

"No, he wouldn't have. And knowing Brittany, she wouldn't have taken a castoff."

"I think she would have taken him. She . . . well, I think she loves him. Or at least she thinks she does. I mean, how can you ever really know until you've spent time alone with a person?"

"Then maybe they'll hook up after tonight."

If she survived . . .

She had to. She had to be okay.

Sitting on the blankets, Rafe moved closer to me and skimmed his fingers along my cheek. "She'll be okay. She's been preparing for tonight—working out, eating right. She's in great shape. She'll handle the change just fine."

He was right. I had to believe that. I didn't want anything to ruin our first night together as mates. I shoved all thoughts of Bio-Chrome and Brittany and the outside world to the farthest corners of my mind. Tonight was mine—mine and Rafe's.

He swept in for a kiss, and I stopped him with a hand to his shoulder. "You can read my mind," I said. "When you're not in wolf form."

"Yes. True mates are always in tune, regardless of the form they're in. Concentrate and you'll know what I'm thinking."

It was a little difficult to concentrate on his mind when his mouth was doing such wicked things with mine. He was kissing me more deeply than he ever had. It was as though he wanted to brand me as his—but the full moon had already accomplished that. It had forced me to choose, and I'd chosen him.

We tumbled onto the mound of blankets. With so many of them piled up, they were more comfortable than I'd expected. Rafe held me close, our arms and legs intertwined. The robe I'd been wearing became nothing more than a blanket to cover us. Skimming my fingers over his bare chest and shoulders, I wondered if his skin was as sensitive as mine.

"Yes," he murmured before he came in for another kiss.

Once again I tried to focus on his thoughts rather than on the kiss.

Silky . . . warm . . . mine . . . forever . . .

He was lost in the awe of it all, the wonder of us. I let my thoughts go, let everything go until there was nothing except us.

I felt much stronger the next day when Rafe and I packed up and began our journey back to Wolford. He was certain the Dark Guardians would be gathering there. Lucas had sent out word. We needed to begin preparing for our battle with Bio-Chrome.

We traveled slowly, taking our time. We wanted to remain in this blissful state as long as possible, because we knew hell would soon be nipping at our heels as we faced Mason and his father. I knew my parents would be at Wolford, waiting to officially welcome Connor into the family.

Surprise! I finally listened to my heart and not yours.

My parents were probably not going to be pleased with my choice, but something had happened as a result of my transformation—or maybe it had happened before, when I'd finally found the courage to make my choice. I felt as though I'd come into my own. I loved my parents and wanted to make them proud of me—but no longer at the cost of my own happiness. If they didn't accept Rafe as my mate, well, then they'd lose me.

It was the pull of destiny, the call of wild beast to wild beast, but I knew I belonged with him.

Near twilight a couple of days later, we arrived at Wolford. We went through the front door into the foyer of the mansion. I tensed as my mom and dad emerged from a hallway.

"Hey, Mom. Dad. You know Rafe."

My mom did the weirdest thing. She smiled and hugged Rafe as though he were a long-lost relative. When she stepped back, Dad shook his hand.

"Connor explained . . . ," Mom faltered.

Dad finished. "He said . . . well, he confessed that he didn't truly love Lindsey in that way. Inconceivable! All these years it seemed as though he adored you. Sometimes you just never know about a person."

Sometimes you don't even know about yourself.

"Speaking of Connor, do you know where he is?" I wanted to see him, just for a moment, to know that he was all right.

"He and Lucas are in the library talking with the elders again about this Bio-Chrome situation."

"What about Brittany? Has she come back?" I asked.

Reaching out, Mom straightened the collar on my shirt, as though I needed to be sharply dressed to stand up to the news she was about to deliver. "No, no one's heard from her."

I felt a pain so sharp that Mom might as well have slapped me. "Have they sent out anyone to look for her?"

"They have no idea where to look."

She sounded so damned calm—as though I'd simply asked her to change her blouse.

"That's no excuse." The idiocy of *no one* looking for her! Not even her mom? Then I remembered that her mom had gone to Europe. Bad timing on her part. How I refrained from shouting was beyond me; maybe the shift had caused me to mature. "She has to be in the forest. We start at one end and we sweep through to the other. She could be hurt, suffering because she went through the transformation alone. Or, God forbid, Bio-Chrome might have her."

I didn't want to say out loud that she might also be dead. I absolutely did not want to go there.

Rafe put his arm around me and drew me up against his side. There was strength and comfort in his gesture. "I'll talk with Lucas, see what we can do about looking for her. We'll find her."

He briefly brushed his lips over mine in reassurance

before saying good-bye to my parents and heading toward the library to find Lucas.

"He seems like a nice young man," my mother said.

"He is," I assured her. "He's totally awesome. And I love him more than I thought it was possible to love someone."

"We always thought you and Connor—"

"I know, Dad," I said, cutting him off. "But see, it's always been my decision, my choice. I chose Rafe."

Dad gave me a warm smile. "Well, at least now I have someone who can keep my car running."

"You have more than that, dear," Mom said sternly. "You have someone who can make our daughter very happy."

I couldn't have been more stunned if she'd suddenly announced she wasn't a Shifter.

"Oh, don't look so shocked," she said. "I was young once. Someday I'll tell you about all the hoops your father jumped through to win me."

"I can't wait." But I also couldn't wait to see Kayla or Connor—or to figure out what we were going to do about Brittany.

After hugging my parents and making plans to have dinner with them, I took my backpack upstairs to the bedroom I was sharing with Kayla and Brittany. Kayla was sitting on the window seat when I walked in. She hopped up, ran across the room, and hugged me.

"I've been so worried about you."

I smiled at her. "I'm fine."

"So you chose Rafe."

I didn't think it was possible, but my grin grew. "Yeah. I love him so much, Kayla. If he doesn't think I hang the moon and the stars, I don't care, because I think he does."

She squeezed my hands. "I'm so happy for you, Lindsey. I sorta always felt like he was the one for you."

"Why didn't you say something?"

"Because it had to be your choice, your decision."

For someone who had just joined our pack, she was learning quickly.

My smile faded. "Have you seen Connor?"

She nodded. "He's going to be okay. So tell me, was the transformation everything you thought it would be?"

I nodded. "And more." I slung my backpack onto my bed. "I'm worried about Brittany, though."

"Yeah, me, too. She just disappeared. No one knows where she went."

"They're not even trying to find her."

Kayla grimaced. "Not exactly true. They're just not announcing it because people are very tense right now with this whole Bio-Chrome mess. They sent a couple of Guardians out to search for her. But they're leaving most of us here just in case we're attacked."

"We should all be looking for her."

"And leave Wolford unprotected?"

She was right—the elders were here, our history was here—but I didn't like it.

"Besides, it hasn't really been that long. Maybe she's just taking her time getting here."

"Maybe." But it didn't feel right to me. Something was wrong. I just knew it.

I walked over to the window and glanced out. Connor was walking toward the forest. I wondered if Rafe's presence had made him leave the library. "I need to go talk with Connor."

I rushed out of the residence and into the forest. Strange, but I caught Connor's scent even though I wasn't in wolf form. I followed it until I came to a small stream. He was standing beside it.

"Hey," I said quietly as I approached.

He glanced over his shoulder. "Hey, yourself. How does it feel to be a full-fledged Dark Guardian?"

"Amazing." I stopped beside him. "Connor—"

"Please don't apologize again," he interrupted. "I've been doing a lot of thinking since the other night. You've been my friend forever. I just always thought we were destined to be together, but the truth is . . . what I felt for you—I'm not sure it was love. Not the kind that

Lucas has with Kayla. And not what you have with Rafe. Believe it or not, I'm really happy for you. I'm glad you found that."

Fighting back the tears, I hugged him tightly. I needed to do that in order to truly let him go. I leaned back and held his gaze. "I do love you, Connor."

"And Rafe."

"Absolutely, I love him, too. And differently. But you're still my friend. You'll always be my friend."

"You'll always be mine, too."

We started walking back to the residence. "I'm worried about Brittany," I told him.

"Don't be. If there's anyone who can survive going through the transformation alone, it's her."

"She likes you, you know."

He shook his head. "Don't even go there. I think I'm going to go girlfriend-less for a while."

"Oh, don't do that," I pleaded. "There's someone for you."

"We'll see. But it sure isn't going to be Brittany."

I didn't say anything, but I knew Brittany could be pretty stubborn. If she wanted Connor, I wasn't sure he'd stand a chance.

That, of course, depended on whether she was still alive.

Later that night, after I'd gone to sleep, I woke up

again. I didn't know why. I didn't know what had startled me. But I had that sense of something not being right.

I closed my eyes and concentrated on Rafe. Then I felt the connection as his mind called out to me: *Miss you.*

Miss you, too. Where are you?

Guarding the perimeter, north side. Join me.

I'm coming.

I'm waiting.

I slipped out of bed. We hadn't closed the curtains. Moonlight spilled in through the window across the beds. I could see Kayla sleeping, but Brittany's bed was still empty. Where was she? What happened to her? I couldn't shake this sense of foreboding that she was in trouble. Big trouble.

In my tank and shorts, I headed out of the room and down the stairs.

Once outside, I started running toward the northern perimeter. I didn't shift, because right then what I needed was to feel human arms around me.

Rafe must have been tapping into my thoughts, because he was in human form, wearing a pair of jeans when I first spotted him. I slammed into him with enough force that he might have toppled over if he wasn't so strong. He draped himself around me, and I could tell he was comforting me.

"Brittany is okay. You need to stop worrying," he

said before I could speak.

"Did you read my thoughts?" I asked.

"Yeah. I'm sorry. I tried not to, but your emotions were so intense that your thoughts kept bombarding mine."

I leaned my head back.

"I can't help it, Rafe. Something is wrong. If Brittany was okay, she'd be back by now. She'd want to show off. She'd be crowing. She survived when no one thought she would. So if she's not here, she's in trouble."

"You don't know that. There could be a hundred reasons why she isn't here."

"Name one."

"It could take her longer to recover. When I went through my first transformation, I ached everywhere. I didn't want to move for about three days."

His words made sense and lessened my panic. Maybe he was right. Maybe I was worrying for nothing.

He skimmed his fingers over my cheek. "You care so deeply. That's one of the things I love about you."

I decided to put my worries away for now. Brittany would return to us and then I'd find out what happened. I'd give her a couple of more days and then I'd insist that we search more diligently for her—that we send out more than just a couple of guys.

But for now, as selfish as it was, I wanted to focus on Rafe. It was time to put him first, to give him my total attention. I told him, "I love everything about you."

His grin flashed in the moonlight right before he kissed me.

I knew the dangers that we had to face were far from over, but for these few heartbeats, nestled within his arms, with his lips playing over mine, I knew that whatever we had to face, we'd face it together.

I couldn't even remember now why I'd ever doubted that Rafe was my one true mate. I desperately wanted for Connor to find his own mate one day. I thought of him now as my first love. There was sweetness in that.

But it wasn't as deep or binding as what I felt for Rafe.

Rafe and I shifted into our wolf forms, his dark fur a sharp contrast against my coat of white.

We guarded the perimeter as the moon began its waning phase. Eventually it would go entirely dark. We'd face our enemies then, during the new moon.

Little did I realize at the time that some of the enemies would come from within.

What I did know was that Rafe was mine and I was his. He had always been my destiny. Nothing would ever change that. Together we would face whatever the future held.